THE DIAMOND CROWN

THE DIAMOND CROWN

V S RAO

Srishti
PUBLISHERS & DISTRIBUTORS

SRISHTI PUBLISHERS & DISTRIBUTORS
Registered Office: N-16, C.R. Park
New Delhi – 110 019
Corporate Office: 212A, Peacock Lane
Shahpur Jat, New Delhi – 110 049
editorial@srishtipublishers.com

First published by
Srishti Publishers & Distributors in 2018

Copyright © V.S. Rao, 2018

Translated from Telugu by Vakkantham Chaithanya

Edited by Preetha Rajah Kannan

10 9 8 7 6 5 4 3 2 1

Printed at Repro Knowledgecast Limited, Thane

Dedicated to Temporau,
the pioneer of Telugu detective fiction, who was
my mentor, and in whose memory
I have created the character
— Detective Tempo.

Acknowledgements

My special thanks to Mr. Arup Bose for selecting my book *The Diamond Crown* and M/s Srishti Publishers for bringing out the same for the reading pleasure of English audience.

Many thanks to Ms. Dipti Patel of WordFamous Literary Agents, for representing my book.

I owe my thanks to Mr. Vakkantham Chaithanya for translating the Telugu version of the book into English, duly maintaining its pace, and heartfelt thanks to Ms. Preetha Rajah Kannan for the expert editing.

And thanks with blessings to my dear daughter Umarji Anuradha for her sincere efforts as an efficient go-between in bringing this book to light.

The car stopped in front of Hotel Everest.

The uniformed chauffeur jumped out hurriedly and, head bowed in deference, held the back door open.

Balaram stepped out of the car in breezy sartorial elegance. He sported an expensive white suit, shiny black shoes and oversized dark sunglasses. The wind rippled his curly hair.

Balaram gave the hotel a perfunctory look before removing his dark glasses. His smug fingers stroked the carefully trimmed moustache, shaped to taper to the corners of his mouth.

The driver closed the car door gingerly, taking care not to make a sound.

Balaram's head jerked towards him: "Idiot, get the briefcase out!" His tone was as abrasive as a rasping metal file.

The hapless driver gave a start and hurriedly reopened the car door. Picking up the maroon briefcase on the back seat, he held it flat on his palms and extended it to Balaram, its handles facing Balaram, so that he could lift it easily. Balaram snatched it from the man's hands and turned towards the hotel.

"Sir, shall I be here at 11.00 o'clock?" the driver asked respectfully.

Balaram stopped in mid-stride. "Come here!" he ordered, without deigning to turn back. Sidestepping Balaram, the driver came to stand obediently before him.

Balaram glared at him with bloodshot eyes, his tie whipping in the wind.

"What did I tell you before we started?" he asked, his voice dangerously calm.

"You asked me to drop you here and to come back at 11.00 o'clock after having my lunch…." the driver murmured.

"So, why do you ask me again? Idiot!" Balaram barked.

The driver lowered his head and intoned, "To confirm… just in case you changed the time…"

"Shut up! Who is to decide whether there is a change in the schedule?"

"You…sir."

"So…you think you are clever enough to give me advice, is it?" Balaram roared, before stalking off regally.

The driver stood still, looking after the tall figure. A sardonic smile flitted across his face. Idiot! He had been paid a hundred rupees that day only to put up with abusive English names: idiot, fool, rascal and what not!

●

The lift glided to a stop at the fourth floor of the hotel. Leaving it to continue its ascent, Balram stepped out alone into the mosaic-tiled corridor. He looked carefully around him, before sauntering to the staircase. It was an article of faith with him to never get out of the lift at the actual floor he intended to reach. If he was headed to the second floor, he would stop the lift at either the third or fourth floor! This habitual little precaution had proved to be a life-saver time and again.

Balaram descended the stairs with a pleasant smile plastered on his face. His furtive eyes, concealed behind the dark glasses, constantly scanned the four directions. He stopped before Room 222. He raised his hand to press the calling bell but paused at the sound of voices inside. Raucous laughter drifted from the room. The door moved when Balaram nudged it with his palm. Fumes of stifling rage consumed him. He sighed resignedly.

Taking a deliberate step back, Balaram gave the door a hefty kick with his left foot. It flew open and crashed against the wall. He burst into the room and slammed the door shut with his back. He glared at the three men seated in the room, like crafty scavengers gathered expectantly around the carcass of a cow. The three heads, which twisted to meet his fierce, red-rimmed eyes, were the hoods of venomous vipers.

Balram covered the intervening distance with long strides. The men rose respectfully to their feet, incipient smiles on their faces.

Balaram locked eyes with them, his own eyes radiating hostility. An uncomfortable silence engulfed the room.

"Why wasn't the door closed and bolted from the inside?" Balaram demanded.

His harsh tone instantaneously snuffed out their smiles.

Parabrahma Rao was the first to recover. His brave attempt at a nonchalant smile revealed a flash of gold teeth fillings. "We kept it open for you, Balaram!"

Balaram walked up to Parabrahma Rao and coolly looked him up and down; the man resembled a skeleton garbed in pajamas and a long shirt. Behind his rimless glasses, Rao's eyes gleamed and darted like quicksilver.

Balaram thought, 'Here is a man who would not hesitate to kill his bosom friend for a quarter of a rupee!' But Balaram had no choice. Rao was indispensable to the success of his scheme. He would have to handle him with the vigilance due to a double-edged blade.

"Nonsense!" Balaram snapped. "You are not on an assignment where you can afford to sit in a room with open doors! Such negligence will ensure that we all land up behind a closed door for the rest of our lives, anxiously chewing our nails!"

"Sorry, Mr Balaram," Rao muttered.

Balaram hissed fiercely at him, "Parabrahma Rao, forget my name. Call me 'Boss!'"

Rao said, "Sorry, Boss!" His crooked, shining teeth reminded Balaram of brass harmonium reeds.

Balaram turned his back to the man and went to the chair at the head of the table. Sitting stiffly upright, he opened his briefcase with a loud click and took out a miniature Sanyo tape recorder.

"Parabrahma Rao," he commanded, "shut and bolt the door from the inside and place this tape recorder against the wall adjacent to the door. Let it play at full volume."

Rao moved to the door with the tape recorder in his lean claws and complied with Balaram's instructions. A western disco number blared out, shattering the room's silence.

Balaram placed a Carona cigar between his teeth; his gaze wandered aimlessly and came to rest on the other two gawking men, as though he had just noticed their presence. The cigar moved in rhythm to his slowly working jaws.

Gajapati returned Balaram's look with moist eyes which conveyed a misleading impression of pervasive innocence.

Balaram took in the other man. Ramjogi sat beside Gajapati with his long, dishevelled hair, his inch-long beard interspersed with the occasional grey. Balaram was not fooled by Ramjogi's lean appearance; he was aware of the strong muscles which rippled beneath the shirt. Ramjogi sat cracking his knuckles through his interlaced fingers, the popping sounds audible above the music of the recorder.

Parabrahma Rao walked back to the table. Before taking his chair, he took a matchbox from his pocket and bent to light Balaram's cigar. Transferring the now-glowing cigar to his hand, Balaram breezily blew out the lighted matchstick in Rao's fingers. Rao again flashed his gold teeth at him.

Clenching the cigar between his teeth, Balaram looked at the trio and started to address them, but stopped short, as the calling bell shrilled above the loud music.

"Ramjogi, open the door!" Balaram commanded.

Ramjogi unlocked the door, quietly pushed it ajar and attempted to peer through the gap, only to jump back in alarm as the door was pushed in forcibly from the outside.

She stormed into the room.

Ramjogi closed the door, his fascinated eyes riveted on her.

She casually tucked her shirt into the jeans which hugged her narrow waist. The thin cotton shirt did nothing to conceal her voluptuous figure. Its top button was unfastened. It was evident she did not wear a bra. The sleeves were rolled up to her elbows in careless elegance, revealing forearms that gleamed like gold. Her shoulder-length hair swayed to her easy gait. Professional dancers could learn a thing or two from the sinuous grace of her movements. The lips, boldly highlighted with red lipstick, were parted to reveal a glimpse of pearl-like teeth. Her long nails, painted a deep red, evoked the claws of a predatory tigress, still dripping with the fresh blood of its kill. Her large eyes came to rest on Balaram. She stopped at the table and smiled at him.

"Am I late?" she crooned. The words caressed the ears like a love song by Asha Bhosle.

"Sit down, Kumkum!" Balaram gestured to a chair.

Kumkum sashayed to the chair in a sensuous explosion of hips and breasts. She leaned back, crossed her elegant legs, took a deep breath and exhaled noisily. She patted her bobbed hair into place.

Parabrahma Rao's eyes were transfixed on her, as though she was a sculpture crafted by his renowned grandfather. Gajapati and Ramjogi mirrored his unabashed interest.

She looked pointedly at Balaram. "Introduce me to your friends, before their heartbeats come to a standstill because of unbearable suspense!" Her smile belied the insult in the words.

The three men burst into a united peal of laughter. Balaram's cigar quivered in his mouth.

"Parabrahma Rao, Gajapati and Ramjogi! You will be meeting Kumkum often from today."

"Why often? It would be better if we could meet her constantly…" Rao's eyes remained glued to her.

The cigar in Balaram's mouth froze.

A Filter King cigarette materialized from somewhere below Kumkum's waist. She placed it between her lips and glanced expectantly around the table.

Parabrahma Rao took the matchbox from his pocket and extended the lighted matchstick towards her. He sat stock-still, staring at the cigarette that took on the appearance of the white stem of a pink flower bud. Kumkum rose and bent forward to light her cigarette from the open flame. The hand holding the lighted stick trembled, as Rao's fascinated eyes locked on the unfastened top button.

Kumkum leaned back in her chair, exhaled the cigarette smoke and looked questioningly at Balaram.

Balaram began, "Gajapati, how is business?"

Gajapati's eyes became even wetter and he smiled bashfully, "Jogging along…." His voice was almost a falsetto.

Balaram turned to Ramjogi, who seemed preoccupied with his knuckle-cracking, "Not bad," he murmured.

The cigar wobbled in Balaram's mouth. "Not bad means not good!"

He looked at Parabrahma Rao.

Rao removed his glasses suddenly, as though struck by something of great importance. He gave the spectacles a vigorous polish with the end of his shirt, before replacing them on his nose and peering through them at Kumkum: "Business is dull…"

Balaram smiled complacently. "I am well acquainted with your state of affairs! I summoned you here knowing well that you have all carelessly burned the candle at both ends and are now groping in the dark. I have in mind a venture which entails both enormous risk and huge money. Would you be interested in climbing on board?"

The trio instinctively turned their attention from Kumkum to Balaram. After all, there is only one thing which can divert a man's attention from a woman – money! Based on past experience, they staunchly believed in Balaram's credentials as a go-getter and a master schemer.

"Parabrahma Rao," Balaram called out, "what's on your mind?"

The cigar in his mouth had burned down to a short stub.

Rao's teeth gleamed. "I was trying to guess the secret behind Kumkum's golden-hued complexion!"

Kumkum giggled.

Balaram gave Rao a fierce stare: "Kumkum applies turmeric to her body before bathing, okay?! Now, answer my question!"

Rao's eyes remained glued to Kumkum as he replied: "Tell us your proposition, Boss. We will go along. We are at our wit's end due to the shortage of cash at our disposal."

Gajapati and Ramjogi sniggered in sympathetic agreement.

Balaram removed the cigar stub from his mouth and looked intently at the three men. "This is an extremely serious matter. It entails walking on a knife's edge. A sword will hang over your heads until the job is completed. If we succeed, you will be set up for life at one fell swoop! But…if we are busted, you will spend the rest of your life behind bars. Two alternatives." He paused. "Take your time before you reply. I will not reveal the actual plan until you have made your choice."

Balaram paused to gauge their expressions.

Kumkum leaned back and gazed at the ceiling as though completely detached from their deliberations.

"You cannot back out once you are privy to the plan," Balaram declared. There was an undertone of menace in his words.

"What does that mean?" Parabrahma Rao asked.

"It means that anyone who is privy to my plan cannot back out. In case he backs out, the plan must be erased from his memory. In fact, it will be arranged for his memory to be permanently erased," Balaram locked eyes with Rao, his lips parted in an ominous half-smile.

Fear gripped the three pairs of eyes. It was clear: once they had given their consent, there could be no retreating with life and limb intact.

Parabrahma Rao was the first to speak. "Alright, Boss. I am in, for better or worse!"

Gajapati and Ramjogi exchanged looks. Then, Gajapati spoke on their behalf, "Count us in, too."

Balaram's face glowed. Biting on the cigar stub once more, he removed four 12" x 10" glossy, coloured photographs from his briefcase, along with half a dozen more in a larger size, and tossed them on the table.

Three pairs of eyes scanned the photos, which featured a gleaming crown. They turned to Balaram in confusion.

Balaram wordlessly extracted some newspaper clippings from the briefcase and added them to the pile on the table. The crown was there again, this time in black and white. Three hands reached out for the clippings. Kumkum examined the colour photograph.

"You can read it later," Balaram said. "First, listen to what I have to say."

They withdrew their hands and turned to him expectantly.

"You may have heard of Dasavatar Baba of Gnana Hill," Balaram remarked.

"Gnana Hill, the one which is sixty kilometres from the city and ten off the main road…is that the one you are talking about?" Ramjogi asked.

"Yes, the same." Balaram smiled.

"It was called 'Blind Hill' in my childhood," Parabrahma Rao remarked. "I suppose that was because it had such a dense cover of trees that it used to be dark even during the day."

Balaram interrupted, "Parabrahma Rao, you are right. 'Blind Hill' is now 'Gnana Hill'." He gave a sardonic smile. "When the hordes of blind followers increase, it becomes *gnana*, the truth! And, thanks to the Forest Department, the trees are not so thick now."

Kumkum giggled and the three men emulated her enthusiastically.

"Of course, we have heard of the Baba. There is much talk about him. It is said that he can convert ash into sweets with his empty hands and create anything from thin air!" Gajapati said.

Balaram laughed. "He can create anything, except currency notes!"

They all joined in his mirth. Balaram stopped and explained, "That is why his devotees offer him many gifts. He has numerous followers, not only in India, but also in America, England, France, Italy and other countries. Several of his devoted disciples and trusted intimates are millionaires—"

"What about the crown?" Rao intervened.

Balaram declared arrogantly, "Parabrahma Rao, your Boss doesn't waste time on irrelevant matters; nor does he overlook the pertinent ones! For your own good, I suggest that you get into the habit of paying attention, without interrupting me with unnecessary questions."

He continued, "Dasavatarananda will soon complete sixty years. On the occasion of his sixty-first birthday, he is to be presented with the crown in the photographs. A crown moulded in gold and studded with diamonds."

There was complete silence and Balaram continued, "Do you know the value of that crown?"

He paused and looked at his associates. The trio stared unblinkingly back at him.

"Two crore rupees!" Balaram announced triumphantly.

"Good god!" Parabrahma Rao hissed in astonishment.

"Its value is next only to the crown fashioned for the deity of the Tirumala Temple, Lord Sri Venkateswara. Mr Fox, who owns diamond mines in Kimberly and Kilimanjaro, has contributed the diamonds for the crown. Many devotees, believing their ailments to have been cured by the Swamiji's miraculous powers, have made liberal donations towards the cost of the gold. Dheerajmal has made the crown free of cost. He believes it is due to the Swamiji's grace that his diamond business runs profitably, without any hindrance from the Income Tax Department. He also credits the birth of a son to his fourth wife to Swamiji's blessings."

"Boss, how did you gather all this…" Parabrahma Rao could not conceal his astonishment.

Balaram gave a self-satisfied laugh. "If you keep your eyes and ears open, you can pick up much information. This news has been the sensation of the week. Reams of newsprint are being devoted to the coverage of the Swamiji's *Shashtipoorti*: the function celebrating the completion of sixty years of age."

"What will the Swamiji do with a diamond-studded golden crown, when he has renounced material goods and lives in an ashram?"

"Swamiji does not wear the crown for his own pleasure. He will do so only for the sake of his devotees!" Balaram smirked and elaborated, "Like devotees feel happy decorating the idol in the temple, the followers of Swamiji feel elated decorating him with the crown."

"I will never understand these crazy devotees!" Rao smiled and threw up his hands.

"Parabrahma Rao, men do these things in order to wash away their sins. They rob the weak and give a share of the plunder to the babas and deities, in the belief that this is expiation for their sins. Dasavatarananda has captivated thousands with his miracles and earned the confidence of his devotees. To them, he is a living god. Their business will come to a standstill without his grace. They will not be cured of their ailments through medicines alone. They will not even bear progeny without Swamiji's blessings."

Kumkum's laughter tickled the men's hearts. Holding a fresh cigarette between her lips, she bent suggestively towards Parabrahma Rao, who hurried to light it with his match.

"In a recent interview to an English magazine, the businessman, Fox, who is donating the diamonds, claimed that it was the ash from the Swamiji's nails which cured him of diabetes." Balaram smiled.

"Nowadays, foreigners are crazy about such things," Rao remarked.

"The blind beliefs of ordinary men are exploited by intelligent men like Swamiji. And now, the blind faith of gullible followers will earn us a crown worth two crores."

"What?!" exclaimed the startled Rao.

"Yes!" Balaram looked into three pairs of eyes blazing with greed, yet tinged with anxiety. "If we work with courage and precision, Swamiji's crown will fall from his head into our laps!"

"Boss, are you for real?" Ramjogi cried.

Balaram stared at Ramjogis' eyes, now as hard as marbles. "Do you think I am saying all this just to pass time?"

"When you summoned us, we expected a good deal, but never did we dream of netting such big fish!" exclaimed Gajapati.

"We too had heard about the crown here and there, but this idea did not strike us," Rao admitted ruefully.

"Parabrahma Rao, not all minds are capable of making plans!" Balaram declared, as he took out a fresh cigar. "Our hands must be poised to make a grab at the opportune moment. The butter made by someone else, through the laborious churning, will now slip into our hands as ghee."

The men's heads nodded like the hoods of snakes to the music of the charmer's pipes.

"Boss, hearing your plan is like listening to Mehdi Hassan's *ghazals*!" Rao gushed enthusiastically.

Balaram's red lips parted in a smile as Kumkum kept her unwavering eyes on him.

"I have a plan to make the diamond crown disappear without anyone being the wiser. This requires that you follow my orders automatically, like robots."

"When crores of rupees are coming our way, we would love to work like robots!" Gajapati enthused, his eyes even wetter than their wont.

"The value of the crown is two crores. Planning is very expensive. Converting the crown into liquid cash also involves much financial outlay. All said and done, I estimate the total expenditure to be fifty lakhs. This leaves us with one-and-a-half crores. I will take 50% as my share for the planning and implementation. You four can divide the remaining 50%

among yourselves. This works out to about nineteen lakhs for each of you."

The four of them succumbed to a fit of nervous, rib-tickling laughter. Gajapati and Ramjogi wiped the sudden sweat from their faces. Parabrahma Rao removed his glasses, wiped them with a handkerchief and wore them again. His eyes flickered from Balaram to Kumkum and back again.

For a few minutes, the music of the tape recorder was the only sound to be heard in the room.

Then, "Boss, how will you convert the crown into such a large amount of cash?" Rao asked.

"Further planning is needed. I must find a buyer who can arrange crores at short notice. We can't trust anyone blindly. We need an individual who would not hesitate to pledge his own mother's *mangalasutra* for money…there are many such unscrupulous people around. Leave it to me!" Balaram was confident.

Rao nodded in agreement.

"I assumed the guise of a press reporter and clicked those photographs of the crown from all possible angles. If our plan is to succeed, Parabrahma Rao must demonstrate his expertise…" Balaram glanced meaningfully at Rao, who looked back questioningly.

"Parabrahma Rao, it is up to you to make an exact replica of the crown, based on the photographs. Can you do that?" Balaram demanded.

Rao picked up the photographs for a closer look. He examined them minutely for a few minutes. He paused to light a cigarette and focused on the photographs once more as he smoked. Balaram took out a palm-sized magnifying glass from his briefcase and wordlessly placed it on top of the photos. With a grateful nod, Rao picked it up and resumed his unhurried scrutiny. Finally, he lifted his glowing eyes to Balaram.

"My father rightly assessed my caliber at the time of my birth; he predicted that I would be the best in my profession. He christened me 'Parabrahma', the supreme lord of the universe. I will now live up to my father's expectations, Boss!" Rao declared proudly.

"Very well! You must make a copy of the crown, using fake gold, and embed it with imitation diamonds. The replica must be the twin of the original."

"Even an imitation costs a lot of money," Rao pointed out.

"You cannot trap an elephant without bait. You cannot buy an insurance policy without paying the premium. Don't worry about the expenditure; you will be provided with everything you need to make the crown. Concentrate on the quality of your work," Balaram assured him with a smile.

"Give me the money; I will buy whatever I need when necessary..."

"Parabrahma Rao," Balaram said resignedly. "I have already made it clear that I am the brain and you are the hand. It is well known that you are an expert in making counterfeit notes. If you go on a shopping spree, your movements will be subject to suspicious scrutiny and you will invite trouble for all of us."

Rao put on an offended air.

"No offence intended," Balaram was placatory. "Parabrahma Rao, not a soul should know about us. Our very breathing should be inaudible to all ears. I will pay you enough money to sit in your workshop and concentrate on your job. If you demand one rupee, I will pay you two, okay?"

The smile returned to Rao's face. He carelessly lifted the magnifying glass from the table and peered through it at Kumkum, focusing on the cleavage exposed by the unfastened top button.

"Parabrahma Rao, watch out! If you look at Kumkum through the magnifying glass, you risk burning your fingers!" Balaram smiled.

Kumkum's musical laughter resembled the plucked string of the *veena*. Rao immediately lowered the magnifying glass and smiled at Balaram.

"Gajapati and Ramjogi, you will open a workshop somewhere underground." Balaram turned to Rao. "You can make use of these two. Kumkum will visit you now and then. Even if you require the rarest of rare components for your work, she will arrange for you to have it."

"There is an underground cellar in my house," said Rao. "It is known to my father, mother and wife, all of whom are dead. I alone, among the living, am aware of its existence. However, it is too dark and there is no air circulation…"

"No need to worry about that! Gajapati will arrange for lights and a fan with temporary electric wiring. You will not need to come out until the crown is made."

Rao, who had lost his wife ten years ago, suggested craftily, "It would be better to have Kumkum stay with us. She can handle the cooking and serving of food, etc."

Kumkum locked eyes with Rao. "Parabrahma Rao, rein in your hyperactive imagination. Cooking and serving food is not my business. And, one more thing… I find your way of looking at me highly objectionable. Behave yourself and stop staring at me!"

Balaram laughed loudly at Rao's discomfiture. Gajapati and Ramjogi joined in his mirth.

Balaram took an envelope from his briefcase and pushed it towards Parabrahma Rao. "The crown's measurements are listed in this, including the inner and outer height, base and peripheral measurements, along with the measurements of the top. It specifies the weight of the crown, and the separate weight of the gold and the diamonds. The number of diamonds is also given. The colours of the diamonds used are listed in detailed order. The photograph at the bottom shows the crown in actual size."

Parabrahma Rao said doubtfully, "It is impossible to make an accurate copy based on photographs alone. I should see the original crown at least once…"

"Forget it!" Balaram was categorical. "That is out of the question. It was deposited in the safety locker of a bank on the day it was made. The concerned bank has put in place heightened security measures for as long as the crown remains in its custody."

Rao heaved a sigh. "Is it enough if it resembles the photo?"

"Good enough! In any case, the photos are so clear that they are mirror images of the original. Don't lower your guard because of this. The difference between the original and your copy should evade notice unless subject to the strictest scrutiny. This will be a work of art, Parabrahma Rao; live up to your name!" Balaram exhorted him.

"I will show you." Rao declared confidently.

"Good. I have full faith in your handiwork. That is why I selected you. You must complete the job in twenty days."

"Twenty days?!" Rao exclaimed. "The time is far too short!"

"That cannot be helped. You pointed out that your cellar is in total darkness. You cannot distinguish between night and day. So, work round the clock and use these two men as assistants."

Balaram tossed a bundle of hundred rupee notes on the table. Greedy eyes fixed on the table and fingers crawled their spidery way towards the notes.

"That is twelve thousand rupees. Take four thousand rupees each. Parabrahma Rao, this is to meet your personal expenses. Start your work on the day after tomorrow. Make a list of things you require and hand it over to Kumkum. It will be taken care of. Put the photos and newspaper clippings in the briefcase and keep it." Balaram waited expectantly.

Rao eagerly opened the bundle of notes, counted it in short order and distributed the money among the three of them. Taking some paper and a pen from his pocket, he made a list of items he required to complete his job. He then swept the photos, clippings and magnifying glass into the briefcase and shut it.

Balaram smiled. "The three of you, keep in mind that you must not shave or cut your hair from today. It may be necessary to spend time in the ashram, in which case, an original beard will be safer than a false one as a disguise."

Kumkum smiled in her turn and quipped, "Yes, yes. The crown may be a copy, but the beards should be original!"

This elicited laughter from everyone. Parabrahma Rao dropped his list before Kumkum. She passed it to Balaram, who scanned it and returned it to her.

Balaram stood up abruptly and said, "Thanks for coming. Forget about this meeting, the matters discussed and the plans made. Don't let anything you drink loosen your tongues."

"We must not utter a word, is it?"

They all moved back in alarm as Balaram roared, "My advice is for your own good. If you say one word about this, you will no longer be alive to utter another word!"

Balaram's smile was devoid of friendliness and did not reach his cold eyes. It conveyed a firm warning.

"You three may leave now. I will meet you in the cellar on the day after tomorrow," Balaram said.

The three men saluted him and turned to leave. Parabrahma Rao's eyes lingered on Kumkum with many unanswered questions.

"Kumkum, close and lock the door, switch off the tape recorder…and come to the bedroom," Balaram ordered.

Balaram's words answered Parabrahma Rao's questions. Rao turned back mechanically and walked out with his briefcase. The door shut on his back.

About fifteen people sat at a round table with glasses of orange juice before them. The manager of the Gnananand Ashram, Soujanya Murthy, included them all in his smile: Police Commissioner, Ramalingam; State Bank Manager, Subbarao; the diamond mine owner, Fox, and his partner, Rocks; Dheerajmal Dhoka; District Collector, Kanta Rao; RTC Zonal Manager, Kurmavatharam; personal assistant of Dasavatara Swamiji, Mangalam; six representatives from different service centers; local senior citizens, Raghurama Reddy and Jagannadham; and press reporter, Prabhanjan.

Soujanya Murthy coughed discreetly and cleared his throat. "A warm welcome to all the committee members assembled here on the occasion of Dasavataranand Swamiji's Shashtipoorti. Swamiji sends us his special blessings…"

He paused in acknowledgement of the silent nods which greeted his words.

Soujanya Murthy rifled through the papers on the table, peered at them through his rimless glasses and looked up cheerfully.

"I am happy to announce that we will be celebrating Swamiji's Shashtipoorti function on Gnana Hill for three days, starting from the 7th of next month. We estimate that about three lakh devotees from India and abroad will be in attendance. So, it is essential that we make appropriate arrangements for security, transportation and sanitation, covering five days. In this regard, our special invitees today are the IG of Police, Mr Ramalingam; RTC Zonal officer, Mr Kurmavatharam; and the District Collector, Mr Kantha Rao. On behalf of the ashram's Board of Management, I thank them for making it convenient to attend this meeting."

He paused and smiled at the dignitaries.

IG Ramalingam nodded and said, "We will ensure that adequate security measures are in place, with the necessary police personnel posted on Gnana Hill and on the *ghat* road."

Taking his cue from the police officer, Collector Kantha Rao leaned forward to announce, "I will depute the required staff from the concerned department to deal with the demands of sanitation. You are welcome to reach out to me if any further departmental assistance is needed."

It was RTC Kurmavatharam's turn. "From two days prior to the function, to two days after its conclusion – that is, from the fifth to the eleventh – we will arrange for ten buses to carry devotees to the hilltop. Will that be enough?"

"Thank you, that will do for us." Soujanya Rao turned to the IG. "Though we expect only devotees to attend the function, as the valuable crown will be on display for three days, we would prefer some armed plainclothes officers to mingle with the crowd, just as a precautionary measure."

The IG nodded his assent. "When will the crown be brought to the ashram?"

Bank Manager Subbarao announced confidently, "Our bank has taken on the responsibility to ensure that the crown reaches the hill on the sixth. It will come in a closed van, with armed security guards in attendance. We have also deputed bank staff to the Hill to count the daily collection money and send it to our bank every evening in the same van."

"Excellent!" approved IG Ramalingam. "The armed security personnel can be stationed on the road uphill when the crown is transported to the ashram. Where do you plan to keep the crown once the celebrations are over?"

Soujanya Murthy cleared his throat. "We have constructed a strong room on the ashram premises especially for the crown's safekeeping. This was done under the supervision of Swamiji's personal assistant, Mangalam."

"Mr Soujanya Murthy," the Collector intervened, "considering the expected, huge influx of people, it is my opinion that arrangements should be made for vaccinations against the outbreak of disease."

"Yes, I agree with that," the IG said.

"Thank you for the suggestion," Soujanya Murthy said, "but Swamiji's name is synonymous with disease control. In fact, even a cold is unheard of on Gnana Hill. In our celebrated ashram, the devotees will not contract any ailments, particularly as they are here to receive Swamiji's darshan. Vaccination programs will have a negative impact on Swamiji's image and the devotees…"

"Yes," Fox interrupted emotionally, "I'm a living example of Swamiji's miraculous power. The great soul cured my diabetes with a spoonful of holy ash. There is absolutely no need for vaccinations!"

Kantha Rao nodded politely and smiled knowingly at the IG.

Soujanya Murthy nodded in vehement agreement. "Moreover, Swamiji habitually sprinkles the holy water from his *kamandalam* over all the food items, including the milk, the idli batter, the vegetables and the drinking water. It is the ultimate instrument of disease control!"

"As you wish…" Kantha Rao smiled again.

Soujanya Murthy beamed with happiness. "Mr Dheerajmal Dhoka, Mr Raghurama Reddy and Mr Jagannadham will supervise the food arrangements. The workers from various service centres will serve as volunteers in the kitchen…"

"Mr Soujanya Murthy," interrupted the IG, "just a second. What was that about the daily collections in the ashram?"

"Swamiji will wear the crown every evening for three days from Shashtipoorti day, when he delivers his speech. At that time, it is customary for the devotees to offer him their donations. At other times, the crown will be kept on display in the hall, where again, the devotees are free to offer their gifts.

Moreover, several lakhs of people who are served breakfast, coffee, lunch, dinner and snacks, free of cost, will not be comfortable with accepting charity. That is why we have put up *hundies* at strategic locations. Devotees can drop their voluntary contributions into these collection boxes and eat their fill with an easy conscience. In addition to this, Swamiji's photos, books, lockets, rings, amulets, etc., will be sold in large quantities as mementoes."

Bank Manager Subbarao elaborated, "Our bank is prepared to count and clear the collection. The amount will be deposited daily in the ashram's account."

Prabhanjan, the journalist, came to his feet. Soujanya Murthy looked at him questioningly.

"When such large crowds gather, there is always the possibility of unfortunate incidents taking place. What precautionary measures have you taken to prevent crimes and accidents?"

"We have requested the IG to set up police outposts at regular intervals. The police force, Home Guard and volunteers will work round the clock. We do have a telephone connection in the ashram. However, recognizing the need for additional lines, we have arranged for the telecom department to set up a temporary telephone exchange on the hill, and also a post office."

Soujanya Murthy paused and looked around with a complacent smile.

"Have you covered all the health and medical contingencies, Mr Soujanya Murthy?" the Collector asked.

"I object to vaccination programs, but all other necessary measures have been implemented. I will give you an outline of our preparations. Although we expect three lakh visitors, we have made arrangements for five lakhs. Twenty-five camps have been erected within one-and-a-half kilometre radius, equipped to house three lakh people in temporary sheds, with drinking water and sanitary facilities.

"We have constructed five large dining halls, each with a seating capacity of one thousand. All precautionary measures are in place to prevent water contamination and wastage. The use of disposable plates and cups will preclude the need for washing.

"A hospital with twenty-five beds is attached to each camp. These will be manned by 250 doctors and a thousand nurses, who will be assisted by about one thousand staff volunteers. Several pharmaceutical companies and foreign firms have donated medical supplies. In fact, totally free medical treatment will be available for any ailment on Gnana Hill during that one week.

"Another piece of good news is that in line with Swamiji's instructions, a temporary maternity hospital will function to meet any emergency. This facility was requested by several female devotees who became pregnant through Swamiji's intercession. About two dozen women expect to become mothers during this period."

"It looks like you have covered everything," Prabhanjan said approvingly. "But, I think there is one contingency you have overlooked. What about unforeseen crimes?"

Soujanya Murthy smiled mockingly. "I think our Crime Reporter, Mr Prabhanjan, sees everything from the criminal angle."

There was general laughter. However, the Police Commissioner and the Collector did not join in the mirth. Prabhanjan rose to his feet. His sombre glance took in all the faces gathered around the table and came to rest on Soujanya Murthy.

"Mr Soujanya Murthy, my presence is not required to cover your conference, or the function; a news reporter would be sufficient to do justice to that. My Editor has deputed me here with a specific objective in mind. He wishes to report the arrangements made for the security of this gathering of lakhs of devotees, where the collection will run into crores..."

"Very well. I have already mentioned the establishment of police outposts and regular patrols. However, I admit that this is only a matter of form. We are confident that no crimes, such as theft and murder, will occur in Dasavatarananda Swamiji's presence. Just as the notorious robber Angulimala was redeemed in Gautama Buddha's presence, a thief will become a gentleman and a murderer will embrace non-violence in Swamiji's presence. Don't worry!"

Soujanya Murthy's confident assertion met with enthusiastic applause from his listeners.

Prabhanjan waited for the claps to subside and smiled sardonically. "Let's hope things go on as smoothly as you predict."

"They certainly will! Keeping in mind the huge numbers of devotees and foreigners expected, we have implemented adequate security and medical measures. But, speaking from past experience, these will remain superfluous. Lakhs of gallons of pure water springs from the rocks uphill and flows down to join the river at the foot of the hill. This 'Gnana Teertham' reaches twenty-five townships including Gnana Nagar, Ramakrishna Nagar, Ramanuja Nagar, Aravinda Nagar, Ramana Nagar and Ramateertha Nagar – all bearing the names of spiritual leaders. This pure, holy water is beyond contamination. This is the reason we are immune to diseases," Mr Soujanya Murthy declaimed in one breath.

"Is there anything else you think we should be aware of?" IG Ramalingam asked.

"I would like to give a detailed account of all the arrangements in place so that we can expect full cooperation from your side."

Soujanya Murthy began to list the preparations in elaborate detail.

Kumkum, wearing blue jeans and a striped shirt, nonchalantly pushed open the door and entered the comfortably air-conditioned room. The door slammed shut behind her. She bolted it and turned to the room's occupant.

A man reclined like Lord Vinayaka on the foam padded mattress of the couch and smiled at her. Kumkum took the soft chair at the foot of the couch. The man's eyes gleamed at her, lust lurking beneath the surface of his shallow smile.

"When I see you, I remember Kumkum in a Hindi film I watched at the age of twenty-five," he said. His voice resembled the croaking of two frogs singing a duet in the rains.

"Thanks. I thought it would be me you remember when you see me!"

The caustic note in her voice amused him greatly.

Then, all levity gone, he asked authoritatively, "What's up? Are things moving?"

"Yes…moving and poised to reach the goal," she quipped.

"Good. Can we trust him?"

Kumkum locked eyes with him. "Isn't it a little too late for that question?"

He nodded in agreement. "You are right. We have paid generously to secure his loyalty. But, there is no need to worry; he cannot ditch us for anyone else. He will be dead if he tries to betray us. As a precaution, I have arranged for someone to shadow him."

"Why do you ask me about his trustworthiness, then?" Kumkum asked petulantly.

"When it is a matter of crores, and the initial expense itself runs into lakhs, surely it is natural to double check things? Alright, tell me…what is the present state of affairs?"

He sat upright and lit an India Kings cigarette.

"The wolves have mingled with the sheep…"

"Tell me in plain words!"

"The four of them have joined Swamiji's disciples. They have blended in seamlessly with the devotees. Four beards cannot be distinguished from among thousands. The Shashtipoorti function is scheduled to begin the day after tomorrow. Balaram says that the plan will be executed at the opportune time. Two of them will first reach the foothills…"

He intervened to ask, "You will also be there, right?"

"Don't you want me there?" she threw his question back at him.

"I got into this because of my faith in your abilities. You must keep him in check until the job is done!"

"He is aware of the reason why I am sticking to him like adhesive tape. Don't worry! We get the goods and he gets the money, that's it!"

He started to say something, but thought better of it. It was safer to keep a few things up his sleeve. He had his own plans for the diamond crown.

"Okay, Kumkum. I will wait for you on the day after tomorrow," he said and stubbed his cigarette in the ashtray.

"I need some money," she said softly.

"Everything is free on Gnana Hill." He smiled.

"Only food is available there," she said in exasperation. "I need more."

He expelled his breath noisily like the blower of a furnace. "How much?"

"Twenty-five thousand."

"What?!"

"Twenty-five thousand," she insisted and bent to pick up a cigarette from his pack. She coolly inserted it between her red lips.

"Nonsense!" he protested. "What will you do with twenty-five thousand in an ashram where people apply ash on their skin? Do you plan to burn the place down to ashes?"

"It is not to gather ash for my skin! I am exposing myself to great risk. It is remuneration for that." Kumkum smiled.

"But…twenty-five thousand! It's too much."

"Twenty-five thousand is nothing but ash to you, in comparison to the price of your diamond crown!" Kumkum laughed.

"You certainly do know how to strike while the iron is hot." He guffawed. Taking a couple of hundred-rupee bundles from under his pillow, he threw them into her lap.

Kumkum came to her feet, picked up the money and put it into the leather purse on the table against the wall. She flashed a smile at him, her teeth shining from behind the red lips.

"Day after tomorrow then!" she said and turned to leave.

"Not just the day after tomorrow. I have been waiting eagerly for you since this morning, Kumkum," he said. Placing his ledgers on the floor, he patted the space on the couch beside him.

Kumkum's disgusted eyes took him in. He looked like an inflated rubber doll, with his hairless chest. The lust in his beady eyes was unmistakable.

"I am sandwiched between two partners, and the bed also comes into the scheme of things!" she complained.

His face hardened for a moment. Then he relaxed; a smile broadened his face.

"In this venture, Kumkum serves as the sword of sex! Come on, be a sport!" he urged.

Flinging her leather bag on the table once more, Kumkum walked towards the bed.

'This gunny bag is giving me lessons in sex, is he?' she thought. The two men were unaware that she was not merely a 'sex sword,' but also a two-edged blade, slashing at both Balaram and him.

Balaram looked down at the rows of people teeming like ants from the temporary camps which had mushroomed on the hill almost overnight. His face reflected the smug satisfaction of an eagle peering at a brood of chicks from its perch on a tree.

The visitors making their way to the ashram from all directions moved in serpentine queues. The spectacular crown was on display in the main hall, the Ananda Mandiram. The devotees circumambulated the diadem in regulated circles.

Balaram complacently stroked his inch-long beard. He peered through his rimless glasses, searching the crowd. Parabrahma Rao merged into the throng like a goat into the herd. Kumkum was immersed in her group. They would surface only when the time was ripe. It was Balaram's idea that they should not be seen together and avoid drawing attention to themselves. Deliberating on his scheme, and its implementation, Balaram pulled out a cigar from his shirt pocket and chewed on it.

Everything had fallen into place perfectly till now. He had been astonished at Parabrahma Rao's skilled handiwork. The replica looked better than the original! The first phase of the plan was over. The second, third and fourth phases should follow in quick succession. Procuring the crown, getting out of Gnana Hill and evading all suspicion, these were the remaining phases. Balaram sighed. The second and third phases were fraught with danger. Someone or the other constantly stood guard over the crown. This called for a diversionary tactic. Again, nobody was leaving Gnana Hill these days. The buses went downhill empty. They could travel downhill in the buses, but it was risky, Balaram told himself. People would be sure to remember if anyone left the hill on Shashtipoorti day. Balaram smiled. He had a plan to safely reach the foothills. He glanced at his watch and slowly descended the stairs.

The minutes dragged like hours as he waited. Continuous announcements blared over the megaphones which numbered over a hundred. The announcers' use of Telugu, Kannada, Tamil and Hindi, along with English, indicated that Swamiji's devotees hailed from all those states and spoke those languages.

The public address system announced that lunch would be served in ten minutes. This was what Balaram had been waiting for, though not because of any desire for the sumptuous fare. He was not in the least hungry!

The hall in which the crown was kept on public display was now closed for the lunch hour. The crowds hurried to the dining halls. Balaram looked at them disdainfully from his position on the bottom-most step of the staircase. The milling crowd reminded him of a herd of cattle blundering towards the pasture the instant the barn doors were opened. Food and sex can make a man oblivious to all else, he thought.

Balaram tried to locate Parabrahma Rao. Though he was not in sight, Balaram was confident that he would show up at the right time and place. Balaram moved forward. He walked past the lines of men who sat satisfied before plates heaped high with food. He made his way through volunteers hurrying to and fro with plates and buckets. His keen eyes soon found what he sought. He quickly picked up a packet of salt from the table, hid it inside his shirt and made his way out. The volunteers, engrossed in serving the food, and shouting instructions to each other, did not pay any heed to Balaram. He went to the dining room's rear entrance.

Balaram was glad to see the place deserted. Within twenty feet of the door stood a cart, which had been pulled uphill by a solitary ox. The unharnessed animal stood nearby, resting and contentedly chewing cud. There was no sign of the cart's driver. Balaram was confident that the man would not return for an hour, as he was busy in the dining hall. He was also certain that the milk cans would be handed over to the store only after the man returned from his lunch.

Balram smiled balefully at the ox which rested with half-closed eyes, like a *bairagi* in meditation.

Balaram waited impatiently on the verandah. Where was Parabrahma Rao?

His eyes lighted on Rao as he came out of the dining hall, wiping his mouth. His teeth gleamed on seeing Balaram. Balaram did not return his smile. He glanced meaningfully at his wristwatch and back at Rao. Avoiding Balaram, Rao turned left and walked away.

Parabrahma Rao reappeared on the verandah after five minutes. He held a large tray, heaped with Mysore jasmine flowers. His beaming countenance hovered over the mountain of flowers. His broad grin held a world of meaning. Balaram locked eyes with Rao as he came closer. Rao's eyes gleamed.

"Swamiji has ordered that these flowers be kept in the hall, and the old ones removed," Parabrahma Rao faithfully reproduced the words he had rehearsed with Balaram.

Balaram took one jasmine blossom from the tray, turned and walked away. Rao followed in his footsteps, tray in hand. They descended the stairs to the hall. The people coming from the dining halls looked respectfully at the flowers. The enthralling fragrance of Mysore jasmine pervaded the air.

Balaram stopped at the threshold of the closed room which was festooned with garlands of flowers. Two men, dressed in saffron robes, with long beards and robust physiques, stood guard. They looked questioningly at the newcomers and the tray with its mound of flowers.

"Swamiji's close disciple, Nanjundappa, has sent these flowers from Mysore by plane. Swamiji has instructed us to remove the flowers spread under the crown and replace them with these," Balaram explained respectfully.

The two disciples nodded appreciatively at such devotion. One of them turned to knock softly on the door, which was immediately opened a crack. Another bearded face peered from behind the gap. Balaram repeated his story.

The guard on the inside nodded and threw open the door. Balaram and Parabrahma Rao entered the room, holding the tray together. The guard shut and bolted the door.

When the guard's back was towards them, Balaram quickly extracted a Mysore jasmine flower from his shirt pocket.

Parabrahma Rao looked on in amazement as Balaram extended the flower towards the guard, saying, "Swamiji said to give this to you with his blessings."

The disciple received the flower with his cupped hands and touched it to his forehead in reverence. Under Balaram's watchful eyes, he raised the flower to his nose and deeply inhaled its fragrance. Immediately, his eyelids drooped. Balaram moved quickly to catch him as he swayed. Seating the unconscious guard in a chair against the wall, Balaram picked up the flower which had fallen from his nerveless fingers. In its stead, he took another flower from the plate and threw it into the man's lap.

Balaram knew that the man would remain in his trance-like state for another five minutes, more than enough for Balaram to finish his job.

He turned his attention to the diamond-studded crown, on its bed of red velvet, with the satisfaction of having reached his goal. He walked to it quickly, followed mechanically by Parabrahma Rao who was still dazed by the latest developments.

Balaram lost no time in getting to work. He removed the crown and set it aside on the table. He swept its place clean of flowers. Taking the Mysore jasmine on Rao's tray, he made a soft bed for the fake crown, which now stood revealed on the tray. Balaram took the replica and placed it on the fresh bed of flowers, artfully spreading the remaining flowers on the tray around the crown.

He scrutinized the two crowns with narrowed eyes. His gaze shifted to Parabrahma Rao, who gawked at the crowns as if mesmerized. Balaram sneered at his protruding eyes and perspiring forehead.

"Come on," Balaram urged in a low voice, "if we stay here any longer, even you will not be able to tell them apart!"

"Yes!" Rao's voice was a feeble whisper.

Placing the original crown on the tray, Balaram concealed it under a heap of used flowers. Rao struggled to control the tremor of his hands.

"Let's go!" Balaram said. "Walk carefully. If you stumble, the pot will break and we will lose the honey."

Parabrahma Rao wet his lips nervously and looked stupidly at Balaram. He directed a furtive glance towards the unconscious man seated in the chair, before walking to the door. Unbolting the latch, he pulled the door open with shaking hands. Balaram strode ahead with a confident smile and pulled the door shut behind him.

Parabrahma Rao followed him with newfound respect for the Boss's unwavering courage and poise.

●

Rao passed his tongue over his dry lips and combed his two-inch long beard nervously. He gawked foolishly at Balaram.

"Boss...he...that disciple...is he dead?" he stuttered in a low voice.

Balaram realized the reason for Parabrahma Rao's zombie-like manner. He patted his shoulder reassuringly and said, "Don't worry. The fragrance of the Mysore jasmine sent by Swamiji, energized with mantras, has sent him into a passing state of *samadhi*. This is only temporary; he would have recovered by now. He would also have bolted the door from the inside and resumed guarding the crown, without batting an eyelid, chanting his guru's holy name."

"How do we make our way downhill? The crown..." Parabrahma Rao left his sentence hanging in the air.

Balaram stared fiercely at him. "No more questions! After fifty minutes, take a harmless detour and join the road. Do not go to the tollgate."

"The crown..."

"Just do as I say!" Balaram snapped in exasperation.

Kumkum, wearing a thin white sari and almost transparent blouse, walked to the telephone booth. The man behind the counter ogled her beautiful figure and sensuous gait. She exclaimed at finding the phone free of users and smiled at the man.

"Triple five, double three...number call, local," she said lightly.

He wrenched his gaze away from her with difficulty to dial the number she had given him. His eyes riveted to her again, as he indicated the booth assigned for her call.

Kumkum entered the booth, patting her hair into place. She picked up the receiver and lifted her eyebrows questioningly at the man behind the counter, who continued to feast on her beauty, forgetting the receiver in his own hands. He came to his senses and hurriedly returned the instrument to its cradle.

Kumkum turned her back to him while taking her call.

"Hello, who is this?" A husky male voice asked at the other end of the line.

She did not give a name. "The crown shines brighter on Swamiji's head than when it was on display," she said.

"Good…excellent!" his tone echoed his excitement.

"Have you sent what I requested to the specified place?"

"It has been waiting there for you for the past half hour," his rough voice was ebullient. "Are you coming back?"

"Right away!" she laughed.

"Kumkum, has he managed to get the goods?" the man at the other end asked anxiously.

"Don't talk nonsense!" Kumkum abruptly replaced the receiver and left the booth.

"Three rupees," said the man at the counter.

She quickly settled the bill and left the booth. The attendant looked after her for a long moment; she had not bothered to take the receipt for the bill she had paid.

The open-air auditorium was ablaze with fluorescent lights and draped with colorful strings of serial bulbs. Lakhs of people sat in orderly rows in pin drop silence.

All eyes were riveted on the crimson throne on the flower-decorated stage at the front. The throne was covered in deerskin. The ashram Manager, Soujanya Murthy, climbed the stairs at the rear of the dais and made his way to the mike standing at the front. He looked down complacently on the calm sea of devotees.

"Jai Gurudev! To our good fortune, Swamiji will grant us his darshan in two minutes. Swamiji will wear the diamond crown for the first time on this auspicious occasion of his Shashtipoorti, and bestow his blessings on us all. I request you to welcome Swamiji by coming to your feet and remaining in silence."

The hundred megaphones carried Soujanya Murthy's words to the lakhs of expectantly waiting devotees.

At once, the vast assembly rose as one, in a single wave of motion. The megaphones amplified and spread the Vedic mantras, being recited out of sight. The ladies walked to the dais in a sedate procession, bearing the *poornakumbhas*. The spectators gazed unblinkingly at the scene, as if to etch it in their memory for all time. The glittering diamond crown soon made its appearance, as Swamiji Dasavatarananda walked to the dais in quiet dignity.

"Jai Gurudev!" Soujanya Murthy cried passionately into the mike. The call, taken up by the humongous gathering, seemed to reach up to the sky.

Swamiji, wearing saffron robes, stopped before the throne and flashed a brilliant smile at his devotees. His teeth gleamed like ivory between his parted, red lips. The silver *trishool* in his left hand sparkled under the stage lights.

Dasavatarananda Swamiji raised his right hand in blessing.

At once, cries of "Jai Gurudev!" shattered the awed silence in the auditorium.

Swamiji settled himself on his throne and the audience resumed their seats. The bearers of the poornakumbhas descended from the dais. Two saffron-clad disciples, stationed on either side of Swamiji, commenced fanning him with silk hand-fans.

"*Om Namah Shivaya, Om Namo Narayanaya,*" Swamiji's opening chant pealed confidently across the vast auditorium, as he launched into his speech. His extempore spiritual discourse teemed with Vedic sermons and quotations from the Upanishads.

A disciple in saffron robes stood with folded hands before a mike stationed in a corner of the dais, translating Swamiji's Telugu words into English.

Swamiji's inner circle of disciples and special invitees, such as the IG of Police, the District Collector, four Superintendents of Police and other officers, Dheerajmal Dhoka, who had made the crown, and his family members, senior citizens, Raghuram Reddy and Jagannadham, Bank Manager Subbarao, Kilimanjaro diamond mines owner, Mr Fox, and his partner, Rocks, sat in places of honour in the front row. About a dozen reporters occupied the press gallery.

Mr Fox was engrossed in the translated version of Swamiji's lecture. He basked in the satisfaction of having donated the valuable diamonds which now adorned the crown on Swamiji's head. He secretly hoped that Swamiji would publicly acknowledge his contribution and bless him on the dais. Fox's eyes remained glued to the magnificent crown, as he listened to the speech and continued his rumination. Suddenly, Fox blinked, and stared harder at the crown. He hurriedly took his silk handkerchief from his pocket, removed his spectacles, gave the glass a vigorous polish, and peered at the crown once again. His heart raced. He looked at the crown, his mouth now agape and eyes starting from their sockets.

Rocks, struck by the sea change in his partner's demeanour, leaned towards him and asked in a low voice, "Is something wrong?"

Fox remained transfixed by the crown. His lips dry, he whispered: "Yeah, something's wrong. The crown glitters too much…real diamonds do not sparkle like that!"

"What?!" Rocks exclaimed in the same low whisper.

"I fear…" Fox stopped and nudged his partner's elbow with an unsteady hand. "Rocks, I must have a closer look!"

Aware that his partner was a globally acknowledged expert in diamonds, Rocks nodded wordlessly.

Turning to Soujanya Murthy, who sat on his other side, Fox place his trembling hand on his shoulder, leaned close to him and whispered urgently, "It's an emergency. I must talk to you in private."

Soujanya Murthy, engrossed in Swamiji's lecture, stared uncomprehendingly at Fox. Fox was visibly upset and was sweating profusely.

Soujanya Murthy feared that he was suffering from some heart ailment. "Mr Fox, is something…"

"Come on, we must talk confidentially! At once!" Fox urged him.

Fox signalled his partner to remain in his chair and pulled himself up with a hand on Rock's shoulder. Comparing the agitated Fox to a housefly floundering in the holy water, Soujanya Murthy too rose to his feet. The two men bent low and hurried from their places.

After crossing the dais, Soujanya Murthy stopped and looked interrogatively at Fox, "Mr Fox?"

"Let's go into the office room," Fox said peremptorily.

Soujanya Murthy followed him with a helpless shrug. Fox closed the door of the office room, leaned back on it and wiped his profusely perspiring face with the handkerchief from his pocket.

"Mr Fox," asked the anxious Soujanya Murthy, "Shall I summon a doctor?"

"Mr Soujanya Murthy," Fox blurted, "I suspect that Swamiji is wearing a fake crown."

Soujanya Murthy's eyes widened in abject disbelief.

"What?" he cried in his native Telugu, his English forgotten in the sudden rush of panic.

"What?" echoed Fox, unable to understand him.

"Are…are you…are you serious?" Soujanya Murthy stammered.

"I am not joking. I am certain about this," Fox said in somber earnestness.

Soujanya Murthy blanched and sank to the floor. His bewildered eyes roved unseeingly over Fox.

Fox rushed across to bend solicitously over him and asked in his turn, "Shall I summon a doctor?"

Soujanya Murthy shook his head in negation but pointed his trembling fingers at the jug of water on the table. Fox hurriedly poured a glass of water and handed it to Soujanya Murthy, who emptied it in a gulp and looked up in complete bafflement.

"What is to be done now?" Soujanya Murthy again lapsed into Telugu, to Fox's utter confusion.

"What?" Fox asked in exasperation.

Soujanya Murthy repeated his question, this time in English.

"First, we need to confirm my suspicion. Let me have a closer look," Fox said agitatedly, patting the magnifying glass in his pocket.

Soujanya Murthy slowly pulled himself together and rose to his feet. "Come, you can observe it at close quarters from behind the throne," he suggested.

In five minutes, they were back in the same room. Fox sank into the chair in front of the table and lighted a John Players Special cigarette, ignoring the no smoking rule on Gnana Hill. Sounjanya Murthy himself was beyond paying attention to such niceties at that moment.

"What do you say now?" he questioned Fox anxiously.

"The diamonds are undoubtedly fakes. And I suspect that the gold is some imitation metal!" Fox seemed to be talking to himself.

Soujanya Murthy sank weakly into another chair. He stared at Fox, at a loss for words.

"In the land of the Vedas…who would think…" Fox was visibly upset. He turned to Soujanya Murthy and barked, "Don't just sit there…do something!"

"I am thinking," Soujanya Murthy spoke like an automaton.

"Enough thinking. Act!" Fox retorted angrily.

Soujanya Murthy rose decisively, strode from the room and closed the door behind him.

Fox puffed furiously at his cigarette and gazed at the coloured photograph of Dasavatarananda on the wall. He repeated mechanically, "In the land of the Vedas…"

●

The Inspector General of Police, Ramalingam, stood in the middle of the hall like a pillar, his face as dark as a thundercloud. Four Superintendents of Police stood at attention before him. Fox and Rocks looked on impassively. Soujanya Murthy gave his agitated account of the developments. He appealed to them to recover the original crown.

"Mr IG," Fox urged, "you must act at once to nail the culprit."

IG Ramalingam nodded and turned to the SPs. "Mr Dayanidhi, Mr Vasudev, erect barricades at the tollgate. From now, no one, on foot or in a vehicle, should leave the hill, irrespective of whether he carries any luggage!" he commanded authoritatively.

"Yes, sir," the two SPs said in unison.

"Keep this under wraps. Only our staff should be kept in the picture. Any individual attempting to leave the hill is to be arrested immediately and brought to the guesthouse near the temple," he instructed them further.

The SPs saluted and hurried to do his bidding. The IG turned to the two other SPs. "I suppose the speech will go on for another hour. It will be followed by *bhajans* in praise of god and then by *bhojan*. This gives us a timeframe of about three hours; we can safely count on having two-and-a-half hours in hand. During this time, every individual, and every piece of luggage on the hill, must be subjected to strict scrutiny. Search everything…search everywhere!"

"Yes, sir," they chorused, as in a duet.

"How many of our men are stationed here?" the IG asked.

"Around two thousand, sir," SP Kartikeya answered.

"Excellent. Let one hundred men form a cordon around the auditorium. Leave only one means of exit from the auditorium to the dining hall. Search every individual, but do not question anyone. Use your eyes...not your mouths!"

"Yes, sir!"

"Another thing, search the ashram premises too. Kitchen, store room, gunny bags of rice and pulses...don't overlook anything. The water tanks too!"

"IG sir..." Soujanya Murthy intervened.

The IG lifted his eyebrows quizzically.

"Whatever we do on Gnana Hill must be brought to Swamiji's notice...his permission is essential before we make a move."

The IG's eyes narrowed. "But, Swamiji is in the middle of his lecture!"

"It doesn't matter. His permission is a must! Moreover," a faint hope tinged his words, "he may discover the culprit with his third eye..."

IG Ramalingam swallowed the laughter which threatened to spill over. "It will be good for all of us if that happens! If he can show us where the original crown lies now, it would save us all a lot of time and energy. Please go and obtain his permission. And also ask him to extend his lecture for at least another hour. We need all the time we can get."

Soujanya Murthy hurried away. The two SPs lingered, uncertain whether to go or stay.

"The original crown has been substituted with a replica. This indicates that this is a well-planned, premeditated conspiracy," the IG said thoughtfully.

"Yes, sir," SP Kartikeya agreed.

"Only an individual in possession of the accurate measurements of the crown could have executed this plan, which suggests the involvement of an insider," the IG continued.

"You have a point there, Sir," agreed SP Rangaraj.

The IG looked around thoughtfully and sat down in a chair.

Mr Fox approached him, with Rocks following him like a shadow.

"Mr IG, you state that more than two thousand policemen are posted here. I find it hard to believe. I strongly feel your department should have taken more precautionary measures."

The IG looked up and asked sharply, "Who says we have not been cautious?"

Fox held his eyes. "The counterfeit crown says that you have not been cautious enough."

"Mr Fox, you should know better. We are doing our level best."

"You are going about things as a matter of routine. You have not taken any extraordinary measures." Fox's voice grew loud and harsh with suppressed rage. His face reddened.

The IG rose slowly from his chair. He locked eyes with Fox and enunciated in cold anger, "Mr Fox, hold your tongue! Your criticism is just empty blather."

Before Fox could retort, the door flew open and Soujanya Murthy hurried in.

"I have acquainted Swamiji with the developments. He has granted permission for us to proceed with our plans," he announced.

"Mr Soujanya Murthy, please confine Mr Fox to a chair. He is obviously highly perturbed," the IG said sarcastically.

"I have contributed a fortune in diamonds.... in the land of the Vedas..."

"Mr Fox, please stay calm," Soujanya Murthy pleaded. He turned to the IG.

"Mr Fox has donated diamonds worth one crore. His emotional reaction and anger are certainly justified. It is but a natural expression of his helplessness and anxiety."

"Of course, we have not donated any diamonds. But, we too are emotionally overwrought, stressed and anxious, Mr Murthy," the IG said pointedly.

He turned to SP Rangaraj, "Do as I said. Search every inch of the garden – under the trees, in the woods, beneath the rocks. Do not leave a stone unturned." He paused.

"Prabhanjan is in the press gallery. Send him here to me. I will be at the guest house in half an hour. Please report to me every five minutes."

"Yes, sir," said Rangaraj and left immediately, along with Kartikeya.

●

"Come in, Prabhanjan," the IG welcomed the reporter.

Prabhanjan looked interrogatively at him.

The IG gestured for him to take a chair. The reporter listened wide-eyed to the IG's story.

"The crown which was on display in the morning, and the one which Swamijii is now wearing, look alike." Prabhanjan smiled. "When Swamiji suddenly changed the subject of his discourse – he is now in the midst of a lecture on the sin of theft – I was surprised at the sudden shift in direction. The reason behind his speech is clear enough now!"

The IG smiled. Soujanya Murthy moved closer to them and said, "Swamiji is extremely kind-hearted. He never loses his temper. He said that he would talk about the sin of robbery in order to bring about a change of heart in the thief. I would not be surprised if we recover the stolen crown before Swamiji concludes his lecture…" his voice trembled in intense piety.

The IG and Prabhanjan exchanged wry glances.

"Prabhanjan," the IG asked, "what do you suggest?"

"Mr Prabhanjan…" Fox began, but was silenced by a gesture from Soujanya Murthy.

The IG gave Fox an irritated look before turning back to Prabhanjan.

Wordlessly, Prabhanjan pulled the telephone towards him. He listened to the dial tone for a second and then called a certain number.

"Detective Tempo," a voice answered at the other end of the line.

"Namaste, Guruji. This is Prabhanjan."

"Do you have a crime to report…Crime Reporter?" Tempo teased.

"Almost certainly. You are needed urgently at Gnanaparvatam. You must come with the speed of wind."

"What's the matter? Murder?" asked Tempo.

"No."

"What then? Has someone planted a bomb to assassinate Swamiji?"

"No, nothing like that. We are faced with a catastrophe. You must come immediately."

"Hmmm. Has someone stolen Swamiji's diamond crown?"

"Good heavens! How did you guess?"

"Once you eliminated the first two possibilities, this was the only one which remained. If anyone planned a robbery on Gnanaparvatam, the diamond crown would be the best pick, right?"

"You have measured the length of the small intestine before we even managed to get in a yawn! Please do come. The IG is also here, waiting for you."

"I will be there in half an hour, unless I am delayed by some untoward accident."

Prabhanjan replaced the receiver on its cradle and turned to the IG. "Detective Tempo will be here in half an hour."

"Excellent." The IG continued, "You grilled Soujanya Murthy's brain the other day with your 'criminal mind'...now, you have got your own back."

Prabhanjan smiled ruefully. "It is the diamond crown we need to get back!"

"Yes," Fox cried passionately, "the diamond crown!"

The IG took a cigarette from his pocket and said, "Let's go to the guest house."

Detective Tempo took a last sip of coffee and put down the cup. He took a cigarette from his pocket and paced the room in deep thought.

The IG, Soujanya Murthy, Fox and Prabhanjan looked at him expectantly.

Tempo stopped abruptly to ask, "Mr Murthy, when was the crown on public display?"

"It was on public display from 6 in the morning to 6 in the evening. We closed the hall during the lunch break – from 12 to 3 in the afternoon," replied Soujanya Murthy.

"When was the crown brought here?"

"Last evening. We brought it from the bank under a tight security cover. We kept it in the ashram's strong room last night."

"We may take it that the crown which was displayed was the original. If it was a replica, Mr Fox would have sniffed out the substitution the moment he saw it." Tempo smiled.

On hearing his name, Fox raised his head like a snake. He looked questioningly at Soujanya Murthy, who translated Tempo's words.

Fox's face reddened in anger, but his words, "You bet!" also resonated with pride.

"Mr Fox, did you take note of the crown in the hall last evening?" Tempo asked in English.

"Unfortunately not. If…" Fox started to say.

"If Mr Fox had chanced to see it in the evening, he would have noticed if the crown was a replica. According to me, the original crown was replaced with the replica during the lunch break," said Tempo.

"Yes," agreed the IG. "Prabhanjan and I are of the same opinion. No one could have made the substitution under the eyes of the public."

Tempo turned to Soujanya Murthy. "Mr Murthy, did you ensure strong security arrangements for the crown during the lunch break?"

"Mr Mangalam locked the door from the inside and stayed on guard in the room himself. Mr Vedananda and Mr Satananda guarded the door from the outside. All three men remained at their stations throughout the lunch break," Soujanya replied.

"Please call them," Tempo said. He stood aside, deep in thought.

Mangalam arrived in a short while.

'Mr Mangalam. Did anyone enter the hall during the lunch break?'

"No."

"Do you mean to say you remained on guard there during the entire lunch break?"

"I did not move an inch from my chair. And I did not let my eyes wander away from the crown for even a fraction of a second," asserted Mangalam.

"Who carried the crown before Swamiji wore it?"

"I was there, along with six important disciples of Swamiji's: Mr Fox, Mr Rocks, the IG, the Bank Manager, Mr Subbarao."

"Mr Fox, did you examine the crown then?" Tempo asked.

"I'm sorry…Swamiji looked into my eyes…I was enthralled and oblivious to everything else. I…"

"Very well…never mind." Tempo turned to the IG.

"Mr IG, the crown was substituted either during the lunch break or at the time Swamiji prepared to wear it."

Tempo addressed Mangalam once again, "Mr Mangalam, please think again. Are you certain that no one entered the hall while you were on guard during the lunch break?"

"I saw no one," Mangalam replied emphatically.

Tempo walked up to lock eyes with him.

"In that case, Mr Mangalam, it is you who substituted the replica for the original crown."

Mangalam's eyes mirrored his hurt. "Mr Tempo, this is an insult. I have served Swamiji for the past fifteen years. I have not committed this sin…it is beyond me!"

"Then, who was the sinner? Either you know him…or you have seen him. Who was it? Tell us! There is no need to be afraid. Tell us who it was," Tempo persisted relentlessly.

Mangalam stared back helplessly. Everyone's startled eyes were on Tempo.

The door flew open and Soujanya Murthy entered, accompanied by two saffron-clothed disciples.

He indicated the duo to everyone and said, "These men know what happened."

"Two men came with a tray filled with Mysore jasmine flowers around 2 o'clock. They said that Swamiji's disciple, Nanjundappa, had sent the flowers from Bangalore and Swamiji had ordered them to scatter the flowers under the crown. I knocked on the door and Mangalam opened it. I passed on Swamiji's orders and he allowed them into the room," one of the disciples explained.

"No…what nonsense! I protest. This is blatant injustice!" shouted Mangalam anxiously.

Tempo turned towards him and the IG sauntered close.

Mangalam blanched and his eyes became bloodshot. His lips quivered.

Tempo addressed the two disciples: "What happened then?"

"The men came out after five minutes with the tray; it was now filled with withered flowers. One of them pulled the door shut. We waited for Mangalam to lock the door, but we did not hear him fasten the bolt. So, I nudged the door and called out to him. He then came and locked the door," Vedananda elaborated.

"Lies, again!" shouted Mangalam.

Tempo ignored him and continued interrogating the duo. "Were the men known to you?"

"No," said Vedananda ruefully. "With thousands of volunteers and disciples pouring into the hill daily, it is impossible to be familiar with everyone. We assumed that they came from Bangalore with the flowers."

"Could you describe them?" Tempo asked.

"One fellow was tall, fat and muscular. The second was slim and about my height. Both had slight beards," Vedananda said thoughtfully.

"Mr Soujanya, it is evident that Mangalam is lying. Let us interrogate him in our own way." There was an underlying menace in the IG's soft voice.

"Just a moment," Tempo intervened. "Clearly, Mangalam is not telling the truth...but, at the same time, I am not certain that he is lying."

The IG cast a bewildered look at the detective.

"If Mangalam is guilty, it is only unwittingly. If he was the real culprit, he would have attempted to divert suspicion from himself. He would have lied by saying that someone did enter the hall while he was on guard. Whatever occurred has played out without his knowledge."

"How?!" exclaimed the astonished IG.

"He has forgotten whatever it was that he witnessed or did."

"How is that possible?" the IG quizzed the detective.

"I suspect that he had been mildly drugged. You are aware that some drugs erase all short-term memory. The victim is not even aware that he has been duped. We do not know how much time the drug bought the perpetrators of this hoax."

"Hmm, I see..." the IG sank into a reverie.

Sathananda's eyes gleamed in sudden recall. "We clearly heard them telling Mangalam, 'Swamiji said to give this to you with his blessings'."

Tempo gave the IG a smile pregnant with meaning.

"So, we can assume that Mangalam was administered the drug through the supposedly 'blessed' Mysore jasmine. Since this flower is unavailable in our area, Mr Mangalam's suspicions were not aroused by its strange scent."

"Mr Tempo, your argument is founded on sound logic; please continue," said Prabhanjan.

"This particular flower was lying at the foot of my chair. I have it here in my pocket." Mangalam took out the flower and handed it over to Tempo.

Tempo gave it a cautious sniff and said, "There is no indication that this is anything but a normal flower."

He turned to Vedananda. "Where did they go with the dried flowers?"

"I think they made for the kitchen and cowshed. I did not pay much attention."

"Mr Soujanya, get a flashlight. We will first search the yard behind the kitchen," said Tempo. Prabhanjan followed him.

They were back in five minutes. Tempo's hand was filled with Mysore jasmine. All eyes rested curiously on the flower.

"This was found in the dustbin, along with the remainder of the withered flowers. By comparison, it is obvious that this one particular flower is distinct from the others. I am certain that this is the flower used to administer the drug to Mangalam. The culprit has been careful to take this flower with him and dispose it off in the bin." Tempo smiled knowingly.

"Mr IG, we need a list of all the vehicles and devotees who went downhill from 3 p.m. onwards."

"Do you think they have already made their getaway?" Soujanya cried anxiously.

Tempo retorted, "If you had stolen the crown, would you sit here with it in your lap?"

Soujanya nodded somberly.

"Our men are on the job now, but no results as yet," said the IG.

"The crown's thief would have made himself scarce much before news of the robbery became public knowledge. He would not wait for us to begin our search," Tempo pointed out.

"Tempo is well versed in a criminal's psychology," Prabhanjan said approvingly.

"Very well. What shall we do now?" the IG asked.

"Let us start our enquiries at the tollgate," Tempo suggested.

"Mr Tempo, we did that before your arrival. The gatekeeper categorically declared that except for the bank van, no other vehicle has crossed the barrier."

Tempo smiled. "It appears that the gateman has been sitting with his eyes closed!"

"What?!" exclaimed Prabhanjan and the IG in one voice.

"A bullock cart went downhill," said Tempo.

"How do you know this?"

"A bullock cart was overturned on the roadside, with its axle broken, and a dead ox lying beside it. The cart's yoke pointed downhill, which makes it clear that the cart met with an accident on its way downhill. The cart was clearly making its return journey from here."

"Did you stop to examine it on your way up, Mr Tempo?"

"Yes, I did. I got down from my car. There was a person lying unconscious on the roadside beside the bull. He was alive. I carried him here in my car and left him with Doctor Kunchitapadam."

"Mr Tempo, your information is mind-blowing! But…why did the tollgate keeper lie?" the IG wondered.

"We will have to find out."

Tempo looked quizzically at Soujanya, who responded, "Mr Tempo, what did the accident victim look like?"

"He was short and fat…weighed more than a quintal. It was a gargantuan struggle getting him into the car! He sported a large moustache and wore a loincloth, vest and turban," Tempo described the man.

"That is Guravayya! He supplies milk free of cost to the ashram on all festive occasions. He is the salt of the earth. Is he okay, Mr Tempo?" Soujanya enquired anxiously.

"Only the doctor is qualified to tell us. By the way, I would like to question the person who received the milk from him today and also those who were working in the kitchen and store room. Quick!" Tempo urged, lighting his cigarette.

The detective addressed the IG and Prabhanjan, "There is no doubt that he is the milk supplier. The road was empty except for the bullock cart and this man." He paused. "Show me the containers in which the milk arrived."

Prabhanjan smiled. "Milk is usually brought in cans to avoid spillage."

"Yes, sir," Satananda spoke up. "I saw him bringing the milk in four cans. I have seen him do this on two or three occasions."

Tempo started to question him, but was interrupted by Murthy's arrival with two men in tow.

"Mr Tempo," Soujanya Murthy said, "this is Ramananda. He is the one who took delivery of the milk."

A short, fat man stepped forward.

"Mr Ramananda, in what containers was the milk brought to you?"

"Cans," was the unhesitant reply.

"Did he leave these cans with you?" Tempo questioned.

Ramananda shook his head in negation. "He needs the cans for tomorrow's milk delivery. He transferred the milk into our containers and took the empty cans with him."

"How many cans did he bring?"

"Four, but the milk in one can was spoiled. So, I returned it to him with the spoilt milk."

Tempo gazed up at the ceiling, puffing at his cigarette.

He turned to Ramananda abruptly and asked, "Did you notice anyone else there while you were taking delivery of the milk?"

"I was in the storeroom; many people were coming and going."

Tempo reframed his query: "Was anyone near you?"

"Yes, I just remembered. One fat, tall man was with us. He helped to transfer the milk into our containers. In fact, it was he who noticed that the milk in one of the cans was spoilt," Ramananda said eagerly.

Tempo gave the IG a significant glance. Prabhanjan exhaled carefully.

"Did he say anything?" Tempo asked.

"Yes, he commented that spoilt milk was inauspicious. It would be a bad omen to spill this milk on Gnanaparvatam. I was deeply touched by his devotion towards the holy hill. I was overjoyed to see his fervour," said Ramananda.

"Did you see him again, or at any other time?"

"I remember seeing him twice."

"Very well, you may go," Tempo dismissed the man and requested Soujanya Murthy to supply them all with hot coffee.

Soujanya Murthy left to do his bidding. Tempo gave Mangalam and the other two men permission to leave. The IG warned them not to discuss the developments with anyone.

"Prabhanjan, what do you say?"

The reporter smiled. "Two plus two makes four."

"Excuse me…" Fox started.

The IG's words were a warning, "Don't bother me."

Fox restlessly lit a cigarette.

"Mr Tempo…" the IG began.

"Just a minute…" Tempo intervened. Taking Prabhanjan aside, the detective whispered something into his ears. Prabhanjan hurried from the room.

Tempo stood before the IG with a smile. The IG's eyes expressed his puzzlement.

"What happened to the cans which the milkman took with him?" Tempo asked.

"Are you implying…" the IG murmured.

"The milk in one can was deliberately spoilt so that he could safely conceal the crown in that can."

"But, how do you make that assumption?"

"There was an empty packet of salt with the discarded flowers. Salt was used to curdle the milk."

The IG puffed at his cigarette in bewilderment. "Mr Tempo, are you implying that the man, or men, carried the cans all the way downhill manually?"

"I will answer your question in a short while."

Sounjanya Murthy arrived with the coffee.

"Excuse me," said Fox, his hands touching Tempo's in pleading.

"Yes?" Tempo asked pleasantly.

"I was unable to follow you. What have you deduced? I beg you to tell me," Fox implored.

Tempo gave him a patient briefing, bringing him up to date with the developments. Mr Fox's countenance bloomed with happiness and admiration. He took Tempo's hands in both his own and gushed. "Bravo...marvellous...great going. My dear Sherlock, keep it up!"

Sipping his coffee, the IG grimaced and rolled his eyes.

Tempo released his hands from Fox's grasp and turned to Soujanya Murthy. "Mr Murthy, consult Dr Kunchithapadam and tell us how the milkman fares."

Soujanya Murthy came to stand beside Tempo. "I forgot to tell you that the doctor is here to listen to Swamiji's discourse. I had a chat with him. He says that the milkman had been given a drug overdose. He will remain unconscious for another hour. He also made it clear that even after he recovers consciousness, he will remain oblivious to events of the recent past. That is the effect of this particular drug, I forget its name."

Tempo turned to the IG. "The same drug was given to Mr Mangalam. That is why he was unable to remember what had transpired."

"I see! Mr Tempo, tell me where have the culprits vanished to?" the IG asked.

"I cannot say where they have vanished, but I can imagine *how* they vanished." The detective took a deep pull at his cigarette.

"After reaching the foothill, they had another ten kilometres to reach the main gate. I very much doubt that they could have walked all that way, especially as they were burdened with the milk cans, one with the crown in it! Obviously, they would lose no time in making good their escape. They could have used the milkman's bullock cart, but they ignored this option. Why?" Tempo wondered.

"Why?" the IG echoed.

"They had access to a means of conveyance which was faster than the bullock cart."

"That's impossible! No other vehicle went downhill today."

"Okay, tell me then, when they left the milkman and his bullock cart on the roadside, why did they not discard the milk cans?" Tempo prodded.

The IG looked to him for the answer.

"We can safely assume that those cans contributed to their disguise as milkmen! Once there was no longer any need to dissimulate, they would have thrown away the milk cans, and got away with the crown."

"Your reasoning is fantastic…but there is one gaping flaw in it! What did they gain by their disguise? Who was taken in by their masquerading as milk suppliers? No vehicle went downhill."

"Aren't you forgetting the bank van?" Tempo smiled.

The IG jumped up. "Good heavens! They wouldn't dare. Travelling in a van which was under police security?! I don't believe it."

"If I had stolen the crown, I would have done precisely the same. When a pilfered crown is worth crores, it makes eminent sense to use a vehicle under police protection. It is the safest course to choose. After all, you would search for your stolen purse in everyone's pocket, except your own. Isn't that true? The policeman's pocket is the safest place for a thief!" Tempo smiled.

The IG nodded thoughtfully. "You may be right, but…"

"Let's verify my hunch. Mr Murthy, I think the Bank Manager is here listening to Swamiji's lecture. Please summon him to this room," Tempo ordered Soujanya Murthy and leaned back comfortably in his chair.

Manager Subbarao hurried in with Murthy.

"Mr Subbarao, who went down in the bank van this evening?"

"Our accountant, Sivatandavam," the manager replied.

"We need to talk to him urgently, wherever he may be. Find out from him whether he gave anyone a lift while going downhill."

"Out of the question! He was transporting a large collection of cash. He would refuse anyone a lift, even god himself!"

"Well, let's hear it from the horse's mouth, shall we? Call him straight away!"

"Why?" protested Subbarao. "It's an utter waste of time."

"Mr Subbarao, it is you who are wasting our time. Use your phone, not your mouth!" the IG intervened rudely.

Subbarao called Sivatandavam. The accountant answered and the manager questioned him. Subbarao's eyes widened in shock, as he listened to Sivatandavam's reply. He covered the mouthpiece with his hand and addressed Tempo. "He gave a lift to two milkmen. He claims that their cart was broken, the bullock was dead and the debris was scattered on the ghat road. Our van was forced to stop. Two villagers, laden with four milk cans, begged for a lift downhill. They pleaded that they had to hurry to replace the spoilt milk in the can before dark. They practically fell at his feet in supplication. Sivatandavam was moved by their tears and gave them a lift in the bank van."

"Ask him for their description," Tempo ordered.

Subbarao listened attentively to Sivantandavam's words over the receiver and reported: "One man was fat and tall. He was the spokesman who did all the talking and pleaded for a lift. The second man was slim and tall. He remained silent throughout.

"Okay. Where did they get down...ask him!" Tempo directed.

"They got down five kilometres from the city," Subbarao said.

Tempo gestured to him to end the call. Subbarao complied and looked questioningly at Tempo.

"Why did you want me to find out these details?" the Manager asked.

"A routine matter. The police spotted two notorious thieves here. They are absconders in a past case under investigation. On being spotted, they made good their escape in the guise of milkmen. Okay, Mr Subbarao…you may go. Thank you. You had better hurry to attend the lecture. I think it will soon be concluded."

Subbarao nodded and took his leave.

"So, the milkman brings the milk by bullock cart, travelling almost sixty-five kilometres daily," Tempo smiled bemusedly.

"What do you mean?" asked the IG.

"The real milkman brings milk from a village in the vicinity of the foothills. Mr Sivatandavam should have smelled a fish when the imposters claimed to be bringing milk from a place some sixty kilometres away from here."

"You are right, but…"

"However intelligent one may be, one is susceptible to error. Sivatandavam committed one such error, and will probably commit many more in the course of his lifetime," Tempo philosophized.

"Mr Tempo, what now? the IG asked.

"Ask your men to call off their search of Gnanaparvatam hill. It is like beating the bushes after the birds have flown."

The IG prepared to call his men.

"Mr IG," Tempo said. "Let's get to the city as fast as possible. Hurry, there is no time to be lost!" He walked rapidly to the door.

"Very well. I will alert my men on the way," the IG fell into step beside the detective.

Mr Fox stood up. "Mr Tempo, what do you plan…"

Tempo gave him a pleasant smile. "Don't worry, Mr Fox. As for you, you are going to sit with Swamiji in peaceful meditation."

With this parting repartee, Tempo strode from the room, the IG close at his heels.

Fox glared at his partner, Rocks, murder in his eyes.

●

Tempo took the driver's seat and the IG settled down beside him. The detective raised a cigarette to his lips.

"Mr Tempo, Prabhanjan…" the IG reminded.

"He will be with us soon," Tempo replied.

Tempo glanced at his watch. The public address system amplified Swamiji's words. Swamiji was attempting to establish that stealing was a grave sin, founding his treatise on quotations from the Upanishads.

"*Asteyam* means to desist from stealing others' property…. stealing is…." his voice resonated over the hill.

"Swamiji is under the impression that the thieves who stole his crown are still sitting on the hill," Tempo's voice was laced with amusement.

He started the car and braked to a halt at the tollgate in two minutes.

An SP approached the car and stood at attention beside the IG, who peered out of the window to give his subordinate some instructions. Tempo descended from the vehicle and made for the telephone exchange. He came back in a couple of minutes and started the car.

Kumkum braked to a sudden halt and got down hurriedly from the car, leaving the door open. She headed for the telephone booth. People on the footpath stopped to gawk at her. She entered the booth and firmly closed the door. She scanned the road through the glass door. She made a call and a male voice answered at the other end of the line.

"Hello?"

"It's me," said Kumkum cryptically.

"Yeah…and it's me! So, what's up?"

"The story is nearing its climax. I am on my way home. By the time I get there, everything should be in place," Kumkum said. "And thank you for hiding the two wheeler in the bushes on the hill near the road for me."

"Everything is ready much before your arrival. I haven't seen you in a long while."

"You talk too much," Kumkum slammed down the receiver and then dialled another number.

"It's me," she said again.

"It's me...tell me," the voice said eagerly.

"I just got here. Everything went according to plan."

"But, I am yet to hear from anyone except you. I am worried."

"Don't worry and make your blood pressure shoot up unnecessarily. The news will reach you, so will they."

"Kumkum, I hope the eagle will not devour the pigeon."

"It appears that doubt mingled with your blood in your mother's womb itself. You are suspicious of everything and everyone. See, in a legal business, one partner may cheat another and get away with it. However, in our line of business, one partner will not dare to double-cross the other as he is well aware that this would put both of them at risk of losing everything," Kumkum admonished him.

The other speaker listened in careful silence.

"I'm sure you understand," she said more cheerfully.

"Yes, I understand it like a simple multiplication table. Of course, you will not be cheated," the voice declared confidently.

"No one can cheat me," Kumkum's voice radiated assurance. "I will be there soon."

"Kumkum..."

Kumkum defiantly cut off the speaker and strode out of the booth. She gently wiped her perspiring face with a handkerchief from her bag. The fragrance from the piece of cloth gave her goose bumps. Once she was through, she would take a long bath to wash away that perfume and relax for a while…there would be no rest for her after that. He adored that particular perfume. Its least whiff was enough to inflame him.

She replaced the handkerchief in her bag and looked back at the telephone booth. A man stood there, his eyes measuring her body. He was slim and tall, his white shirt tucked carelessly into his trousers, full sleeves rolled up to his elbows. She gave him an irritated glare. He puffed at his cigarette and smiled at her. She thought, all men are alike. Even the saints on the hill were ogling her with wide eyes. Perhaps this was how Viswamitra gazed at Menaka. Kumkum got into the car and closed the door, looking back at the booth again. The man still stood there, the smile lingering on his face. She floored the accelerator, cursing all males.

The man stood still until the car disappeared from sight. Then, he entered the telephone booth.

He sat on the cot, legs crossed like Lord Vinayaka. He looked like an impatient cat, licking its whiskers over the covered saucer of milk. He stuffed four spoonfuls of Paan Parag into his mouth. Chewing noisily, he lit a cigarette. He was restless. Why had he not returned his call? Had he absconded with the treasure? He rubbed his bare stomach and shoulders agitatedly. What would he do if he was double-crossed? The shrill of the telephone cut through his anxious thoughts. He grabbed the receiver with his elephantine, trunk-like hand.

"Yes," he barked hoarsely.

"Mr Gupta, the consignment will be delivered to your godown. Keep the payment ready." The voice was clear and steady.

A glow of happiness lit up Gupta's face. His eyes glittered like diamonds.

"Hurry!" he replied eagerly.

"Will be there in ten minutes."

"Just a minute...where are you now?"

"There is no need for you to know that."

"Nonsense! I need to know...anyone can tail you and find me here. I don't want that to happen. If you tell me your location, I will give you discreet directions to get to my place," Gupta explained.

"Mr Gupta, no one can teach a hunting lion how to stalk its prey in the forest. Be prepared and ensure that everything is ready."

The line went dead.

His left hand snaked forward to the bottom of the cot and pressed a button. He smoked blissfully. Gupta looked at the individual who materialized silently from behind a thick iron door which slid noiselessly open. The new entrant was taut and tall. A thick coat of coarse hair covered his arms and legs. His feet were those of a beast. His scanty hair was combed back slickly from his forehead. The bushy eyebrows, crawling over his brow like centipedes, met at the center. Long hairs sprouted from his ears, like fans awaiting a breeze. He flashed his yellow teeth at Gupta.

Gupta sighed and beckoned him close. He came and stopped near Gupta, gliding noiselessly over the floor.

"Mangu, we will soon take delivery of some butter. It should be melted in fifteen minutes and its shape completely transformed. Do you understand?" Gupta leered.

Mangu nodded his head vigorously.

"The delivery man must be paid. Do you have the packet ready?"

"It is in a suitcase." His voice was that of a frog croaking under the leg of a buffalo.

"Excellent! Go upstairs and stand at the window. Use the powerful binoculars...observe if only one individual is approaching us, or whether he is accompanied by anyone else. Check that no one follows him into our compound. Come down after ascertaining that he is alone. I will keep him engaged until you return," Gupta ordered.

Mangu moved away mechanically. The door closed behind him and he was gone.

●

Balaram sat down regally on the chair positioned in the room's centre. He wore a white suit. Three clean-shaven men, bare chins gleaming, stood in a row, facing him.

Parabrahma Rao was now garbed in pajamas and kurta. Their faces were bloated with high spirits. Balaram smiled at their happy countenances and stroked his curved moustache with complacent pride.

"I will leave in five minutes. According to my estimate, I should be back with the cash for the goods by noon. You will receive your shares after that," Balaram paused.

Rao emotionally removed his glasses, wiped and replaced them on his nose; Ramjogi grinned from ear to ear; Gajapati's eyes almost dripped moisture.

"Parabrahma Rao," Balaram said seriously, "do not go overboard once you receive your share of the money. Do not make a public display of your sudden wealth. Do not, at any cost, rouse suspicion. At least for the next one year, continue to lead a simple life. Any overt sign of ostentation and we will all be reduced to paupers."

Parabrahma Rao's face fell. "It is difficult to keep a tight rein on one's hands and mouth before a heaped plate of delicacies. I am a person who loves to savour my food."

Balaram gazed somberly at him. "Eat your fruits secretly, in silence. None should see you eating or hear you belch."

Parabrahma Rao lit his cigarette in pointed silence. It was obvious that Balaram's advice did not sit well with him.

Balaram turned to Gajapati and Ramjogi. "Do you intend to heed my advice?" he asked.

Both of them nodded in agreement. "We will live inconspicuously for the next six months. After that, we will move to some distant nook and begin a new life."

Balaram came to a decision. "Very well, Parabrahma Rao. It appears that you will be a glutton and give yourself indigestion if I serve you a full meal at one go. I will give you your share in easily digestible, small portions,"

The cigarette slipped from Rao's fingers and he turned anxiously to Balaram, who remained dead serious, his face showing no signs of levity.

"I'm sorry, Mr Bala… sorry, Boss! I will follow your advice. I will be cautious. Not just for one year, but for two. I will live in the same old pajama and kurta. There is no need for installments. A single payment will do. Please give me my full share today itself!" he pleaded.

Balaram smiled. "I trust all three of you. We have been discreet till now; we should hold on to our discretion until this incident fades from public memory. Don't forget that I will watch you like a hawk. If you spread your wings too wide, I will clip them for you!"

Three pairs of eyes stared helplessly at Balaram.

Gajapati said, "Your advice is for our mutual safety. We will heed your words."

"If you do, you will reap the benefits." He got to his feet. "Wait here until I return."

Parabrahma Rao picked up his fallen cigarette. "Boss, it would be too nerve-wracking to wait here. We will go to my house and wait for you in the cellar. Please meet us there."

Balaram smiled. "That's a good idea. You are too easily excited. I was afraid you would faint when you saw the crown."

He picked up the big leather bag concealed under the cot and said, "After 12.30."

Parabrahma Rao's voice quavered. "Boss, you will come back, won't you?"

Balaram stopped mid-stride. He turned slowly to face Rao and locked eyes with him. Rao's face was drenched in perspiration, his eyes glittering like glass beads.

Balaram said deliberately, "Parabrahma Rao, that is a very foolish question. Of course I will not come back. I will run away with the entire loot, cheating you all. You can become a police approver first thing in the morning. You know everything about me and can share the information with them. Gajapati and Ramjogi can be your eyewitnesses. Then, the police will hunt for me and catch me. They will let you free in return for your help. And you will have the satisfaction of getting even with a backstabber like me…okay?"

Parabrahma Rao remained transfixed, unable at first to comprehend Balaram's diatribe. Then, he hurried to him and clutched his hands.

"Boss, forgive me! I am flustered like an ant at its first glimpse of a mound of jaggery."

Balaram sneered. "Don't live all your life as an ant, grow up!"

Parabrahma Rao looked on anxiously as Balaram strode towards the door. "Boss…."

Balaram stopped again and turned to Rao in exasperation. "What now…?"

"Boss, where is Kumkum? What about her share…." Rao's voice tapered away into silence.

"She will be there at the right time. She will certainly get her fair share. What is it to you?"

"Boss, when a woman has that much money in her hands, it would be good for her to have a man's companionship," Parabrahma Rao leered.

Balaram's eyes were cold hailstones. "Parabrahma Rao, are you planning to offer her your companionship?" he challenged.

Parabrahma Rao gave a forced smile and subjected his palm to calm examination, like a palmist. "After my wife's death, I have lived a solitary life for ten years. Happiness is now suddenly within my grasp. I desire Kumkum's company. I will willingly give her my support. She will agree if you intercede on my behalf." Hope mingled with a strange bashfulness in his voice.

Balaram burst into loud laughter, while Rao stared at him.

"Parabrahma, if you place your faith in Kumkum, you will be reduced to becoming an ash-smeared sanyasi within a month. Forget Kumkum! By the way, do you know the meaning of Kumkum? It means vermillion. Your pockets will soon be bulging with money. Marry some turmeric or collyrium and lead a happy, discreet life. I repeat, forget vermillion!"

Gajapati and Ramjogi joined, Balaram's mirth.

"Boss…" the wounded Rao began.

Balaram cut him off impatiently. "Parabrahma Rao, you are wasting time. You are an expert forger. Authentic women like Kumkum are beyond your reach. It would do you good to keep this in mind."

Balaram left the room with these words.

The car braked to an abrupt halt. Tempo turned to the IG seated beside him. "Get down and stay in touch with me on the phone. I will keep you updated on any developments."

"Mr Tempo, where are you going?" the IG enquired.

"I don't know…"

"What do you plan to do?"

"I don't know…"

"Mr Tempo…" the IG said in confusion.

"There is something I must do…somewhere I must go. If you need a break, make sure someone is at hand to answer my calls."

"Mr Tempo, it would have been best if we had erected road-blocks on the city roads, like we did on the hill. It slipped our minds in the hurry. We assumed the thieves were still on the hill."

"Let it go! It is foolish to lament over water which has flown under the bridge. It would be best if the police continue to keep the theft under wraps. Let everyone think that Swamiji is wearing the original crown." Tempo smiled sardonically.

"Will you…"

"I will try. I will sniff out some clues. I will try to smell a rat," Tempo murmured, rather enigmatically.

"Mr Tempo, I see no clue so far. "

"Every foot has its unique print. No one can walk without leaving footprints," Tempo declared mildly.

The IG descended from the car. "Very well. You follow your nose. I will meet my people and decide on our course of action. I will ensure that I remain available on the phone round the clock."

Tempo's car sped ahead. His eyes scanned both sides of the road. After five minutes, his eyes glittered like diamonds on seeing a man standing on the footpath, beneath a streetlight, smoking a cigarette. Tempo stopped near him and opened the passenger door with his left hand. The man, dressed in white, climbed in and closed the door. The car moved on.

"What's the story?" Tempo asked, his eyes on the road.

"I visited a dozen flower suppliers. Your belief that Mysore jasmine is unavailable in our area was sound. A certain individual placed an order for a large quantity of Mysore jasmine from Bangalore with City Flower Suppliers. The florist arranged for the supply from Bangalore and…"

"Prabhanjan," Tempo interrupted, "who placed the order for the flowers?"

"A woman wearing a transparent white sari, a white blouse…"

Tempo gave a low whistle. "Ahah! Another female member of the gang! We have to search for this woman…"

Prabhanjan cut in with a smile. "I chanced upon a woman in a see-through white sari and white blouse."

"Where? When?"

"I stopped at the telephone booth to make a call. I saw the woman there…and heard her sweet voice."

"Go on!" Tempo said excitedly. "Did you overhear the conversation?"

"I was tired and had to lean on the wall of the booth. I heard one side of the conversation."

Prabhanjan quickly briefed the detective on what he had heard.

"Then?" asked Tempo.

"Then, she left the booth. The expensive perfume she used pervaded the air. I leered at her like a roadside Romeo. She glared at me and drove away in a huff."

"What did she look like?"

"One can look at her unblinkingly for days together," Prabhanjan smirked.

Tempo turned to the reporter who continued to smile.

"Bobbed hair. Very fair complexion like a luscious guava…a jaunty bindi on her forehead."

"Prabhanjan, did you note the number of her car?" Tempo asked urgently.

"I tried, but the car didn't have a number plate."

"Hmmn. That definitely points to something fishy."

"That is what roused my suspicions. I strongly feel that this is the same woman who ordered and took delivery of the Mysore jasmine. She had vanished by the time I reached that conclusion. Without a doubt, she took the left on the main road."

"That's no use to us! We can't find her destination based on her direction. Alright, what about the other details I wanted?" Tempo paused to light a cigarette.

"I checked all the past records of intellectual crimes and studied various cases. There was nothing pertaining to forged jewellery. I tried one last option. There is a man called Nirmalchand, who is an expert at forging and selling duplicate ornaments clandestinely. He has come under the public scanner a couple of times. However, there was no concrete evidence against him. I pretended to be someone who needed to make the duplicate of an ornament and gathered some information."

"What is Nirmalchand's address?"

"Mr Tempo, according to my information, Nirmalchand is no petty pickpocket. He is a big shot who robs banks."

"Very well, Prabhanjan. Go to the IG. Take two constables with you and search all the city roads. If you see any numberless cars, or number one beauty, stick to them like a limpet."

"Fine, and what do you plan to do?"

If you will give me his address, I will meet Nirmalchand," said Tempo.

"Thirteen, Marathee Line 2, Town," replied Prabhanjan.

The Reporter got down and Tempo started the car.

Kumkum pushed open the door and entered the room. The man seated behind the table rose to his feet. He had a dignified bearing and wore the uniform of an Inspector of Police. He sported neat, close-cut hair and a lush moustache. He smiled at the new entrant.

"Ready?" Kumkum asked.

His eyes took in Kumkum's tight jeans and clinging shirt, which emphasized her stunning beauty. Her attractive body was a magnet to his unblinking eyes. He gave a soft whistle. The door behind him opened and two policemen entered. They moved quickly to stand stiffly at attention beside him. Their rigid posture suggested that they had just swallowed a crowbar each! Kumkum gave them a fleeting glance as the inspector said, "Let's go."

Kumkum moved to him and reached out her hand. He took a revolver from the table and placed it on her open palm.

She quickly checked the revolver and placed it in her bag. She glanced at her wristwatch and sank into the chair opposite him with a smile.

"Let's start in six minutes," she stifled a yawn behind her hands.

"One hundred and twelve, bring Miss Kumkum tea," he ordered, without looking up at the constable. His eyes continued to feast on Kumkum.

●

Parabrahma Rao sat in an old chair in the wide basement and looked thoughtfully at Ramjogi and Gajapati. He heaved a sigh.

"I say it is unfair of Balaram to order us to remain seated at the table without partaking of the feast laid before us," Rao complained abruptly.

Gajapati and Ramjogi nodded. They empathized with his sentiments.

"Balaram lived like a king yesterday, he lives like a king today, and he has the chance to live like an emperor from tomorrow. As for us, we have been living like beggars and he wants us to continue living like beggars in the foreseeable future. We are being deprived of comfort in our lives. We are expected to live like a eunuch married to a wife like Rambha. This is blatant injustice!" Rao spat out his words between clenched teeth.

"Yes, Boss's attitude does not make any sense," Gajapati sang the same tune.

Rao looked at him mockingly. "Really? Then, tell me, why did you keep your mouth shut and nod your head like dumb oxen?"

Gajapati protested half-heartedly. "Parabrahma Rao, you know we do not have the courage, or the intelligence, to oppose him."

Ramjogi added, "If we had supported you, he would have threatened to dole out our shares in installments too." He paused. "By the way, to be fair, I think he has a point…"

"Leading a dog's life, without enjoying the benefit of hard-earned money, is utterly pointless! What is the point of possessing wealth and still living like beggars?" Rao persisted.

"Let's pretend to agree to his proposal and go along with him. Once we get our hands on our shares, we can live happily as we wish," Gajapati said knowingly.

"You two are ignorant! We are being unfairly treated on another front. He takes half the money as his share, giving that dame, Kumkum, a generous cut, no doubt. The remaining half is to be divided into three paltry portions for us. When all's said and done, what we get is mere leftovers! He is throwing scraps to us stray dogs!" Rao's words throbbed with jealousy.

The stunned Ramjogi and Gajapati gaped at his outburst.

"We have risked life and limb making the duplicate crown. It is easy enough to make plans in theory. It is a different matter altogether to make a faithful replica. You know how much effort we have put in. In all honesty, we are entitled to equal shares. As for that vamp, Kumkum, all she did was loll on his lap!" Rao snapped bitterly.

Gajapati and Ramjogi exchanged looks and turned to Parabrahma Rao with new insight in their eyes.

"I have a suggestion to ensure that we get a share commensurate to our effort," Rao volunteered.

Two pairs of eyes turned to him in curious anticipation.

"He will come in with money for four of us. Only three of us will go out," a malignant smile lit up Parabrahma Rao's face.

Gajapati and Ramjogi frowned in bewilderment.

Parabrahma Rao came to his feet and moved to them. He gazed intently at them, his lips still parted in a sinister smile. His glittering eyes rivalled the diamonds in the duplicate crown.

"We will leave this room with the money divided fairly and equally among the three of us," Rao's whisper lured them on with its diabolic promise.

"Parabrahma Rao, what about…Balaram…" Gajapati's voice quavered.

"Balaram…" Rao sneered, and continued in cold deliberation, "that jackal who plotted to swallow half the money, and Kumkum, along with her share, will sleep permanently in the soil beneath this floor."

"Good god!" Ramjogi cried out. His face glistened with drops of perspiration.

Gajapati's eyes grew wetter than ever.

Rao declared, "My dear friends, he is a constant threat to us. If we spend an extra rupee, he is sure to jump down our throats. He is absolutely unscrupulous and will not hesitate to go to any length to suppress us. After our spectacular adventure, I cannot tolerate anyone lording it over me."

He continued, "Unfortunately, people like us tend to fall prey to such smart rogues throughout our careers. I speak to you from the prompting of my intelligence. Quick! We do not have time. If you join hands with me, we can get twice as much as what he offered us. We will have his share, and the dame's too. Let your intuition guide you to a golden future built for yourselves with a windfall of lakhs and lakhs!" Parabrahma Rao urged, as he cleverly hammered the malleable iron.

Gajapati and Ramjogi exchanged looks in which greed and fear vied for supremacy.

"We have already been lying low for the past month. Once we have the money, we can move to distant locations. No one will notice our absence, or miss us. No one's suspicions will be aroused by our disappearance," Rao pointed out.

"Parabrahma Rao, how will you finish off Balaram?" Gajapati asked the question uppermost on his mind.

Ramjogi inclined his head in attention.

Rao's eyes glittered at the question, which confirmed their unspoken decision.

He said proudly, "I cut diamonds with ease. So, this will be a piece of cake for me. When his attention is focused on dividing the money, I will send him to his maker in a split second. Leave it to me. There is another room leading from this one. I will leave you there. You must dig a pit with the shovel and crowbar stored there."

Rao moved to the wall. Gajapati and Ramjogi glided close behind him like his shadow.

"He is on his own. No one is following him," Mangu declared, entering the room.

Gupta's face stretched with glee. He rose hurriedly from the cot.

"I will be in the strong room. Bring him there by the stairs. Don't use the lift," Gupta instructed.

Mangu turned on his heels and left to do his bidding.

"Mangu…"

Mangu looked back interrogatively.

"After leaving him with me, bring us orange juice. You know how to make orange juice, right?"

Mangu grinned broadly. He was not one to fritter away his physical energy. He resorted to words only if absolutely essential. He preferred to use his eyes and teeth to convey meaning. After Mangu's departure, Gupta put on a long kurta and hurried to his strong room.

He lit a cigarette and looked expectantly at the closed door. It opened slowly. A tall, dignified Balaram stood framed by the threshold. A complacent smile flickered on his face.

"Welcome," Gupta cried in effusive warmth.

Balaram strode into the room, carrying a black bag. Gupta's eyes were riveted on the bag.

"Congratulations, Mr Balaram! Churning the ocean single-handedly, you have secured the pot of amrit!" Gupta grinned from ear to ear.

"This is not amrit, Mr Gupta, this is Adilakshmi." Balaram moved to the sofa and sat with the leather bag carefully balanced on his lap.

Gupta stared at the bag like a starving cat at a plump rat. "Balaram, show me the goods."

"Now, now, Mr Gupta. You know better than that. You know the rules," Balaram chided gently.

Gupta narrowed his eyes.

"Mr Gupta, I would not be so foolish as to sell you a replica for crores of rupees. You know very well that a duplicate remains in place of the original, and no one has wised up to the substitution yet." Balaram smiled.

"Of course." Gupta turned to Mangu who stood at the door.

"My mouth is parched. Bring us something cool to drink," he ordered, seating himself on the sofa in front of Balaram. His eyes kept returning to the bag like iron filings to a magnet.

Mangu placed two tall glasses of orange juice on the table before them.

"Mr Gupta, is the money ready?" asked Balaram.

"Of course, of course. I have it ready in two large suitcases." He gave Mangu a meaningful glance.

Mangu moved to the wall and touched a particular patterned strip. A steel cupboard was revealed in the wall. Lugging two large suitcases from it, he placed them on the nearby cot. He opened them a crack under Balaram's watchful eyes. Balaram looked with satisfaction at the neatly arranged rows of currency notes.

His cold eyes turned to Gupta. "Mr Gupta, I don't have the time to count the money now. I will take it at face value and count it later. Let me make one thing clear – if even one note is missing, I will take it to be a deliberate affront. I will meet you after that. And, believe me, our meeting will not be a friendly one!"

Gupta's eyes widened in astonishment. "This is a huge amount. I would not derive any benefit from cheating you of one or two notes. I do not cheat my clients."

"That is for your own good," Balaram remarked.

Taking the crown from the bag, he placed it beside him on the sofa.

Gupta stared at the crown with a gaping mouth. His eyes gleamed like pebbles in awe. He rose slowly and sank down on the sofa beside the crown. He stroked the crown with trembling fingers. Taking a lens from his pocket with shaking hands, he peered at the diamonds for a while. Balaram smiled condescendingly at the sweat on Gupta's face.

"Mangu…" Gupta's voice cracked in suppressed excitement.

Mangu came to stand beside him. Gupta handed him the lens. Mangu scrutinized the crown in his turn and returned the lens to Gupta. His teeth gleamed.

"Balaram, the crown is genuine," declared Gupta. He held it up with his two hands. Balaram noted his avaricious eyes with indifference. Gupta looked like a pauper who had glimpsed treasure for the first time in his life.

"Mr Gupta, your head is too large. It cannot accommodate the crown. Leave it," Balaram mocked.

Gupta replaced the crown on the sofa and got to his feet. "Mr Balaram, my throat is dry. Let us have some orange juice." He leaned forward and took the glass in front of Balaram.

"My throat is wet enough," Balaram replied pleasantly.

Gupta smiled at him and Balaram noticed that the smile did not reach his eyes.

"Come on," Gupta urged Balaram in a quavering voice, "let's celebrate."

Balaram stared at the glass in Gupta's hand, and then at the glass which stood on the tray on the table.

"When huge sums of money exchange hands, it is dangerous to accept the hospitality of the other party," Balaram remarked casually.

Gupta looked at him in apparent bewilderment. Balaram noted the change in his face.

"What do you mean?" Gupta asked.

"Money is your lifeblood. I trust that I have made my meaning clear. Let's not waste any time here."

"You are being foolish, Balaram. I regret to say that I am affronted by your doubts and insults."

In the blink of an eye, Balaram snatched the glass from Gupta's hand. With his other hand, he picked up the glass on the tray and poured the juice from one glass into the other in brisk alternation, thoroughly mixing the contents of the two glasses.

Balaram looked mockingly at Gupta's concerned face and extended one glass towards him.

"Gupta, you take the first sip…I will follow suit," he said.

Gupta's hands hung limply at his sides. His agitation was obvious. "You are insulting me."

Balaram smiled sardonically. "I do not want to accept your hospitality and risk losing my consciousness or my life."

Gupta blanched. His lips trembled.

"Come on, drink!" Balaram challenged him loudly. "Drink and prove that you have not mixed poison with the juice."

Gupta's eyes started from their sockets in amplified fear.

Balaram sneered at him. "Gupta, hope and ambition give a man life, but avarice kills him. Unlike you, I am not a millionaire. However, life has taught me much. Grow up! If I don't return in good time, my accomplices will call the police. They will inform them that you are in possession of Swamiji's diamond crown."

Gupta's furtive eyes darted here and there like a rat seeking an escape route from the cat's den.

"Gupta, I am keeping the crown. You will carry the two suitcases like a railway porter and load them into my car. I will throw the crown out once I cross the main gate of your compound. And of course, you will keep this Mangu under lock and key in this room when we walk out."

"No, no," Gupta protested anxiously, "take the money and leave the crown here. I will not come out of this room."

Balaram smiled proudly. "Unlike you, I do not stoop to cheating my partners. I cannot digest the crown…it is money I need. Come on, move!"

As Balaram bent to replace the glasses on the table, he felt the pressure of cold metal against the back of his neck.

"Don't bother to put the glasses on the table. I don't have the patience to mop up your blood from the tiles. Drink the two glasses of juice. Come on, drink!" a menacing voice warned Balaram from behind.

Balaram froze for a second. He looked at Gupta. Gupta's face gleamed with smug satisfaction.

Balaram's eyes shifted sideways to take in the revolver pressed to his neck. The yellow gleam of Mangu's teeth was visible, as was the death lurking in his snake-like eyes.

"Balaram, it is obvious that your throat is now dry. Drink!" Mangu mocked him.

Gupta moved to pick up the crown. Holding it like a helmet, he walked towards Balaram and sneered: "Balaram, you will not go back, nor will your accomplices inform on me. Kumkum would have shut their mouths by this time," Gupta grinned.

The IG rose hurriedly from his chair as Tempo and Prabhanjan entered the room.

"Any new developments?" the IG asked.

"I need to interrogate a person. I require six policemen and Inspector Pruthvirao. If necessary, we will have to take that person into custody," replied Tempo.

"Who is this person?" the IG enquired.

"Nirmalchand. He is an expert in duplicating ornaments. He is a godsend to those husbands who make a practice of replacing their wives' genuine ornaments with replicas, and using the proceeds from the sale of the original to gamble. I have met Nirmalchand," Tempo paused to light a cigarette.

"Is he the one who made the replica of the crown?" the IG asked curiously.

Tempo smiled. "He is a businessman. He does not wield the hammer and the pliers himself. I had a pleasant chat with him. It emerged that one of his past employees is an expert forger. He claimed that it was almost impossible to distinguish the originals from the replicas that man makes. He is a past master in his field."

"Who is this man?" questioned the IG.

"He is no longer working for him. Nirmalchand fired him two years back. This man's fingers are like chisels and his brain is a sharp knife. He is as crafty as a fox. On Nirmalchand's orders, he made duplicate ornaments for a husband who was a big shot, a VIP. This husband kept the replicas in the bank and gave the original ornaments to his mistress. After a few weeks, that fellow met the husband and blackmailed him by threatening to reveal the truth of the substitution to the wife. The terrified husband succumbed to the blackmailer. When Nirmalchand came to know of this, he immediately dismissed the expert forger from his service."

"Mr Tempo," the IG almost shouted in his curiosity, "Who is this man? Where is he?"

"He has three names...but, one house...one address," Tempo said with an enigmatic smile.

The IG frowned. Tempo smiled back nonchalantly.

"I have to question him immediately. Ask Pruthvirao to come at once."

The IG pressed the intercom in studied silence.

●

Tempo parked the car in the shadows and turned to Pruthvirao who sat beside him.

"Pruthvirao, the two of us will enter first. Let your assistants take up position here. They will enter the picture and play their part at your signal."

Tempo got down from the car, with Pruthvirao close on his heels.

The house stood a little away from the road in an old, dilapidated compound. Tempo paused. Darkness shrouded the place.

Tempo nudged the front door, alert for the least sound. The door was locked. The Inspector instinctively put his hand on his revolver. Tempo stopped him with a gesture. They walked silently to the rear of the house and examined the back door.

Tempo again pushed at the door; it did not budge. He pricked up his ears for a moment. Then, taking a pencil torch from his pocket, he examined the door in its narrow beam. A dark bolt held the door shut.

Tempo whispered to Pruthvirao, who handed him a knife. The detective inserted the knife blade into the keyhole, with Pruthvirao playing the part of a lookout.

●

The exhausted Ramjogi and Gajapati, drenched in perspiration, looked up at Parabrahma Rao who stood supervising their labour.

"Another half foot and he will have enough space to sleep like a babe in its mother's womb."

Gajapati wiped the sweat from his brow with his index finger and asked, "Parabrahma Rao, will everything go according to plan? Will he come back?"

"He has to come back. He knows very well that it he does not come back, six hands will put a noose around his fat neck. And one more thing, he kept all his conversations and contacts confidential. But, he underestimated my ability to ferret out even the best kept of secrets. I identified the person he is selling the crown to. I heard him call Gupta 'a blood-sucking leech of a financier'. That gave me the clue. If he double crosses us, he will also be dealt with," Parabrahma Rao gave a sinister smile.

"Come on, another half foot, and then I need to relax," Ramjogi said.

●

Tempo pushed the door open and entered the dark room stealthily, followed by Inspector Pruthvirao. The detective closed and bolted the door quietly. The two men stood like pillars, forgetting to breathe. Their eyes slowly grew accustomed to the darkness in the small hall. The heavy silence pressed down oppressively on them.

Tempo slowly cased the surrounding. Dust covered the room, which was dirty and pervaded by an odour of decay. He stopped at the wall on the left, before a closed door. The detective placed his hand on the door and pushed gently. The door opened with a slight creak. The two men entered the room and shut the door. The Inspector's heavy breathing disturbed the room's ominous silence. Menacing darkness filled the corners. The minutes ticked by. The heat was stifling.

Tempo's hand suddenly gripped the Inspector's. The detective softly walked towards a gleam of white on a black screen which held his eyes.

Tempo stopped before the white spot and rubbed it with the palm of his hand. He took a hurried step back. All his instincts screamed that there was someone in the house. He ran his hands over that section of the wall once more. It was clear: this was no wall, it was a sheet of reinforced metal.

Tempo whispered, "Pruthvi, this is an iron door. Someone is inside. You can see the pinpoint of light through the chink in the metal door."

Both men held their breaths and strained their ears in the silence. A muffled metallic sound reached them.

"Pruthvi…do you hear it?" Tempo whispered.

"Yes," murmured the Inspector.

"Someone is inside. They are busy with something…" Tempo said and pushed the iron door cautiously.

The door did not budge.

"What do we do?" the Inspector whispered.

Tempo contemplated his next move in silence. If they attempted to force the door open, the sound would alert the people inside. There were only two means of exit – the front and back doors. As the front door was bolted from the outside, anyone wanting to leave the house would be forced to use the back door alone.

"Pruthvi, position two of your men in front of the house and another two at the back door. Bring two men here," Tempo softly instructed.

Inspector Pruthvi glided away noiselessly.

Tempo stood listening to the rhythmic metallic sounds that echoed from inside the locked room. The minutes ticked by.

Inspector Pruthvi arrived with his two men.

"Tempo, shall we force open the door?" the Inspector whispered.

"It is impossible to open the door without making a sound. So, let's just knock at it like familiar acquaintances," Tempo replied.

He gave the door a decisive knock.

●

Balaram looked at Gupta and Mangu from the corners of his eyes. Fearlessly, without the least hesitation, he dropped the glasses of juice on the floor. The glasses shattered on the mosaic tiles with a resounding crash.

The next instant, cursing under his breath, Mangu pressed the revolver's muzzle beneath Balaram's ear.

Stoically ignoring the gun, Balaram turned to Gupta and said, "Gupta, you cannot get away with double crossing me. Kumkum is no longer working for you. She is now my accomplice, my faithful shadow. She continued fooling you by pretending to be your emissary. Don't be hasty…"

"Shut up!" Gupta spat at him. "Kumkum would never be so foolish. You cannot intimidate me."

"People who fail miserably through grave errors of judgment are legion. Open your eyes and ears and listen to me. Take your share and give me mine," Balaram locked eyes with Gupta.

Gupta cackled greedily. "I want both. I want the diamond crown and the dough. Mangu will give you what you deserve."

He turned to Mangu. "Mangu, take him away! I do not want this room messed up. You know how to dispose of his body."

Mangu nodded wordlessly and glared at Balaram, a bestial gleam in his beady eyes.

"Gupta…" Balaram's words were cut off, as Mangu lashed out with a backhanded slap to his. Balaram ran his tongue over his split, bleeding lips; his clenched knuckles whitened and his hands instinctively curled into fists. The pressure of the revolver against his ear intensified. Balaram controlled his anger, breathed deeply and loosened his balled-up fingers.

"Hands up!" Mangu commanded between clenched teeth, grinding the revolver against Balaram's neck.

Balaram obeyed.

"Move!"

Balaram moved forward. Gupta waddled to the door and pulled it open. Goaded on by the pressure of the gun, Balaram shuffled forward like a helpless bull. His mind was in a whirl of doubt. Kumkum would await his return for another half hour. She would come in search of him if her suspicions were aroused.

The gun abruptly shifted from under his ear to his back, keeping level with his heart. Mangu pushed him roughly forward. Balaram disdained the skeleton-like Mangu, but what kept him in check was the powerful weapon in the goon's hand and the flash of animal fury which raged in the man's eyes.

"Thank you, Balaram…and, goodbye!" Gupta sneered as Balaram crossed him.

Balaram stepped out of the door, ahead of Mangu. Mangu's hand, holding the revolver, stood positioned firmly between them.

Suddenly, a hand flashed forward from the left and fell on Mangu's outstretched arm with the force of a sledgehammer. The sickening sound of breaking bone was followed by Mangu's shriek of agony. The revolver crashed to the ground with a metallic thud.

The gun which had whacked Mangu's hand now hit him on the chest, the force of the impact throwing him back into the room.

The awed Balaram turned to observe Mangu's fall, only to draw up short as the muzzle of a revolver prodded him menacingly above his heart. Balaram gaped at the stranger in amazement – a fat, tall man with close-cropped hair, wearing a police uniform, stood leering at him. Balaram froze in shock.

"Balaram, the show is over! Move back into the room!" The Police Inspector underlined his command with a prod from his service revolver.

Balaram stepped back into the room to find two policemen covering Gupta and Mangu with their revolvers.

The Inspector roughly ordered Balaram, Gupta and Mangu to stand with their backs to the wall, like prisoners of war. Gupta, in a state of shock, was drenched in cold sweat, his kurta clinging to his obese body. He clutched the diamond crown to his belly with shaking hands.

The Inspector moved to Gupta, took the crown from his nerveless fingers and placed it on the nearby table. His eyes took in the shards of glass scattered on the floor.

He turned to Gupta. "So, you have all hatched a clever plan for the diamond crown!" His smile did not reach his eyes.

Gupta's eyes darted furtively. "Inspector, I know nothing of it. I heard that a diamond crown had been made for Dasavatarananda Swamiji only through the newspapers and magazines. On seeing the crown, I realized that this man had stolen it. Mangu, my assistant, and I, had determined to hand over this thief, along with the crown, to the authorities. You have arrived at the right time…"

Balaram glared balefully at Gupta's concocted tale. His attention was diverted by the Police Inspector's sarcastic peal of laughter.

"Mr Gupta, I have been standing at the door, listening to every word uttered in this room. I believe you want both the crown and the money, right?"

The startled Gupta quickly composed himself. "Inspector, I have not committed any crime. I did not steal the crown. I cannot be held guilty if an individual approaches me with stolen goods. As a matter of fact, what you overheard was me playacting. I did this in order to buy time and keep him here until the authorities arrived. Fortunately, you have come on your own accord. You are welcome to take away the thief and the crown."

The Police Inspector smiled coldly at Gupta, whose dissembling eyes gleamed. He walked deliberately to the suitcases on the cot, opened them and looked pointedly at the bundles of currency neatly arranged inside. He turned back to Gupta.

Gupta swallowed once and muttered hurriedly, "That money is meant for another legal purpose…"

The Police Inspector did not deign to reply.

Balaram stared at the Inspector, who continued to ignore him. Just a half hour ago, not a soul knew that the diamond crown had been stolen. He was aware that Gupta would have posted someone on the hill to keep track of his movements and report the developments. But, how on earth had this police officer uncovered the secret of the theft? Where had this man descended from?

Parabrahma Rao, Gajapati, Ramjogi and Kumkum were the only other people who were acquainted with the conspiracy. Who could have turned whistleblower? Why would they throw mud on their own heaped plates of food? Somewhere, something had gone wrong. Why did this Inspector persist with his crooked smile?

The policeman's ear-splitting whistle recalled Balaram to the present. The door opened. Balaram gaped in open-mouthed astonishment.

●

"Stop!" barked Parabrahma Rao urgently.

Gajapati's and Ramjogi's hands, holding the crowbar and shovel, respectively, froze at his command. They raised questioning eyes to Rao, who listened in intense concentration.

He turned to them with a sinister smile. "Here he comes! Quick! Put aside your tools and wash your hands and faces. I will put our plan into action at the right time. You know what to do next. Come on, let's go!"

Gajapati and Ramjogi followed closely behind Parabrahma Rao as he ascended the narrow stairs. Rao stopped at the landing and listened; a knock sounded on the door.

"Boss?" Parabrahma Rao called out softly. He was well aware that nobody could gain access to the house, except Balaram, who had the key to the front door.

"Come on, open the door!" an impatient voice shouted through the door. "How long must I wait?"

"Not for long," Rao thought maliciously, before releasing the bolt and opening the door. The smile was wiped off his face at the sight of the stranger standing before him.

"Who are you? What are you doing here?" Rao barked.

Tempo silently considered the trio. The tall, slim man confronting him was beardless. The other two men were also close-shaven.

The detective thought quickly…'Veerabhadram… Subbarao…Parabrahma Rao…whom did he want now?'

On the spur of the moment, he said, "Mr Parabrahma Rao?"

"Yes, that's me. What do you want? Who are you? And how did you get in?"

"It's an emergency! You must come immediately to Gnanaparvatam…you may have heard of Swamiji's diamond crown. Our boss, Mr Dheerajmal, suspects that the diamonds embedded in the crown are not authentic. He wishes to have your opinion…"

Tempo paused to look at Parabrahma Rao. His sharp eyes noted the emotions flitting across Rao's face at the mention of the Hill and the crown. Parabrahma Rao frowned at Tempo.

"Mr Rao?" Tempo prodded.

"I…it is not possible for me to come with you now. I am busy. I have other pressing commitments…" Rao stammered.

"Several VIPs await your arrival. They are all aware that you are an expert in this field. The IG of Police has asked me to request your presence on his behalf. Of course, you will be adequately compensated for the consultation," Tempo smiled persuasively.

Parabrahma Rao blanched. Gajapati and Ramjogi could not suppress their extreme agitation.

"Sorry, I regret that I cannot come. I will definitely be there tomorrow," Rao stuttered. How could they possibly have discovered so quickly that the crown was a fake? He was afraid that Balaram would arrive at any moment. He prayed that Balaram would stay away.

Tempo stepped back and smirked at Parabrahma Rao. "Very well, Inspector. Take Parabrahma Rao into custody. It seems he is not willing to come with us!"

Parabrahma Rao trembled convulsively. Inspector! Custody! He gawked at the Police Inspector who held a revolver in his hands, flanked by two policemen.

"You three…come out with your hands on your heads!" the Inspector barked.

Stepping forward, Tempo found the electric switch and turned on the light, dispelling the darkness. Taking his revolver from his pocket, he cautiously descended the narrow stairs. He was back in a couple of minutes.

He glanced thoughtfully at the trio covered by the Inspector's revolver and addressed Pruthvirao, "The cellar is empty, except for a freshly dug pit."

He turned abruptly to Parabrahma Rao and snapped. "Where is the diamond crown?"

Parabrahma Rao quaked and gaped at Tempo. "What… diamond…. crown?"

"I will be more explicit. Where is your boss…the man who smuggled the crown in a milk can, transporting it in the bank van?" Tempo demanded, fixing the hapless Rao with a steely stare.

Parabrahma Rao stood stock-still in shock. He forgot to breathe. His lips quivered. The Inspector's revolver bored into his ribs.

"Talk!" the Inspector shouted.

"Tell me, Parabrahma Rao. Who is he?" Tempo prompted.

Rao was speechless. He reeled under the tremendous shock.

"Who is the pit in the cellar meant for? Is it for your boss?" Tempo asked sarcastically.

"Come on, speak!" the Inspector thundered.

"It's okay, Inspector," Tempo smiled. "His eyes give him away!"

Rao blinked in amazement.

"Inspector, there are some questions which he must answer with his mouth. Let's take him to the headquarters. Use your own methods of interrogation. When each of his nails is plucked out using cutting pliers, Parabrahma Rao will sing like a bird. If necessary, deploy three pairs of pliers and let the three of them sing in chorus. Let's move! There is no time to lose." Tempo guffawed in cold amusement.

Tempo turned to the other two for the first time. Both were pale and one man's eyes were moist.

"Parabrahma Rao, tell them..." Gajapati's eyes grew wetter than ever.

Rao heaved a sigh. "If I spill the beans, will you guarantee that I will not be punished?" he asked.

"We will have to see about that. Now, quick...tell me everything!" Tempo admonished.

"Balaram has taken the diamond crown to Gupta..." Parabrahma Rao began. Tempo had all the information he needed in under five minutes.

"Pruthvi, send a message by wireless. Ask your men to come and take Gajapati and Ramjogi to your headquarters. Stage the arrest with great fanfare."

The detective continued, "Balaram may return at any time. Ensure that enough men are stationed here to give him a fitting welcome with bullets. Rao is coming with us. Tell Prabhanjan to call off the search for the car," Tempo gave his instructions in a quick staccato.

●

The door opened and Kumkum walked into the room. Balaram's heart raced in alarm. Why was Kumkum here? Had she walked like a rat into the trap? Balaram knew that the same thoughts were racing through Gupta's mind.

Hands resting on her slim hips, Kumkum surveyed the occupants of the room. Her face showed no sign of fear or surprise. Her teeth glistened between her parted red lips. Her sardonic smile filled Balaram with a strange dread.

"So, is everything under control?" she asked the Inspector, who laughed complacently.

"Kumkum!" The shell-shocked Gupta cried out.

"Shut up!" Kumkum snapped furiously at him.

Balaram stared at her unblinkingly. Kumkum, she had enacted a drama. She had double-crossed both Gupta and himself. No doubt about it! The bitch had been a police plant and had toyed with both of them. Balaram clenched his fist. How he would love to use it to wipe the smug smile off her face.

Kumkum glided gracefully towards the suitcases. She opened her eyes in wide caricature at the sight of the bundles of currency and said, "It looks like Guptaji had everything at hand…" She gave a sarcastic chuckle.

"This is base treachery," Gupta shouted.

"Really?!" Kumkum sniggered loudly and turned to the Inspector.

"I will take these suitcases as my remuneration. You take the crown, along with this King and this Emperor into your custody," she announced, pointing to Gupta and Balaram.

"No!" squealed Gupta, like a pig being slaughtered. "That money belongs to me. To me alone. Take the blasted crown and the thief and leave me alone with my money!"

"Mr Gupta, you are guilty of buying the diamond crown, which is stolen property," the Inspector declared.

"No!" Gupta protested loudly. "I didn't even try to buy it. It was he who wanted to sell it to me. It's not my fault! You can't prove that I have committed a crime."

"We are aware that you and Balaram together hatched the conspiracy to steal the diamond crown. Kumkum will come forward to give evidence in court to that effect," the Inspector smiled balefully.

Gupta stared at the Inspector like a drowning man desperately clutching at straws.

Balaram looked on with bewildered, bloodshot eyes.

Gupta's eyes gleamed in sudden excitement. Instead of besmirching his name and reputation in court, it would be better to sacrifice one third of his black money. If he managed to save face, he could always make more money later.

"I will give it up!" he declared. "Let me off. Don't involve me in this…"

The Inspector ran his fingers through his short hair and looked thoughtfully at Gupta and Kumkum.

"Accept the deal, Inspector," Kumkum urged with a throaty laugh. "The diamond crown and the thief are yours. You need not bring in Gupta's name. I will also leave him out of it, provided I get my remuneration."

"Okay…" the Inspector nodded slowly.

Balaram was unable to believe his eyes and ears. Obviously, the Inspector would get a cut from Kumkum's remuneration. Gupta, that thief... scoundrel...cheat. He was going scot free!

"Gupta is the mastermind behind the crime. If I am going down, rest assured that I will drag Gupta down with me. I will not remain silent!" Balaram warned.

The Inspector looked at Balaram, who had spoken for the first time, with abhorrence.

"You will not have the opportunity to speak, Boss," Kumkum declared nonchalantly.

"What do you mean?" Balaram cried.

"No one will believe the words of the thief who stole the holy diamond crown of Swamiji from Gnanaparvatam," the Inspector declared.

Kumkum's malevolent smile underlined the Inspector's words.

Balaram was silent. He was tormented by the thought of Gupta cleverly maneuvering to get away scot free, leaving him to face the music. It would come to public notice that he was a notorious thief. He would have to spend the rest of his life under constant police scrutiny.

Gupta grappled with his own demons. Balaram had nothing to lose. A few days of government food and imprisonment, that was all! But, in his own case, all was lost – the advance, and ten million, including the money in the suitcases.

"Inspector, please ask your men to carry these suitcases to the car; they weigh more than Gupta's body!" Kumkum's caustic words scorched Gupta's heart.

The Inspector moved to Balaram, covering him constantly with his revolver. "One hundred and twelve...handcuff this man!"

He locked eyes with Balaram and said, "Turn around!"

Balaram turned slowly. The revolver pressed under his ear. His hands were roughly linked with the click of the handcuffs. The revolver was now at his back. A hand grasped his shoulder and spun him around viciously. The Inspector locked eyes with him.

"So, you are the mastermind, is it?" he taunted. In a blur of motion, his left hand came in forceful contact with Balaram's cheek; the sound of the slap resounded in the room.

Balaram's cheek swelled; blood dripped from his jaw onto his tongue.

Balaram glared furiously at his assailant. "Inspector, you have no right to manhandle me..."

"Shut up!" the Inspector lashed out. "Once we are out of here, I will kick you too...you bastard!"

Under his supervision, the two constables picked up the suitcases. Gupta watched them in an agony of longing. Mangu sighed like a dumb ox.

"Gupta, it looks like your chimpanzee would shed tears on your behalf!" the Inspector smirked. "Remember, mum's the word! If you open your mouth, the prison doors will also open for you. Understood?"

Strange, incoherent, guttural cries emerged from Gupta's mouth.

The Inspector looked at Balaram, who ignored him. Balaram was focused on Kumkum, who studiously avoided his eyes. Why was Kumkum doing this? Did she have delayed scruples? In that case, why was she taking the money in the suitcases? Why? Why?

Balaram had a sudden epiphany. Kumkum was certainly no paragon of virtue. She would not collaborate with the law or the police in that case? Things fell into place. These men were not policemen! Now, everything made sense. The 'Inspector' had not bothered to question him about his accomplices. Kumkum would have told him about them. However, they had changed the original plan. Kumkum was unaware of the fact that they were now waiting at Parabrahma Rao's cellar.

Balaram's heart pounded against his ribs. These imposters would not let the law deal with him; they would eliminate him! For the first time, Balaram broke out in a cold sweat. His heart fluttered like a bird in a tiny cage. Kumkum had cleverly used her body as a honey trap to deceive and cheat him.

"Kumkum…" he called. She turned slowly to face him. Her eyes shone triumphantly like the sun's reflection on the water of a serene lake.

A sparkle caught his eyes. The fake Inspector was placing the diamond crown into its bag.

"Kumkum!" Balaram called again. She faced him indifferently. He beckoned her closer with his head. She came to stand near him.

Balaram gazed into her large eyes. "I trusted you. Why are you doing this?" he asked quietly.

Kumkum noted the bloodshot eyes, swollen cheek and split lips with a careless smile.

Balaram said weakly, "Kumkum, I know he is not a policeman. Let's give him a share. Help me!"

Kumkum widened her eyes in mock astonishment. Her lips parted in a slow smile. Her teeth sparkled like the diamonds in Swamiji's crown.

"Smart bastard! Your eyes are now empty of their former pride and arrogance. I'm glad." She hissed, her eyes jeering him.

She held his gaze for another second, before turning away. As she sauntered past, her proud hips, emphatically outlined in skin-tight jeans, taunted Balaram.

"Gupta!" Balaram shouted. "They are imposters…they are not policemen. They are robbing my money and your diamonds."

He took a couple of hurried steps towards Gupta, who stood still in bewilderment. Mangu's eyes glittered. Balaram realized that Mangu had understood his unspoken message.

The so-called Inspector turned towards Balaram with blazing eyes. As he rushed towards Balaram, a movement caught his eyes. It was Mangu, gliding forward as if on wheels. The 'Inspector' quickly shifted the bag with the crown from his right hand to his left.

Kumkum turned back abruptly. She held a revolver in her hand. In two quick steps, Kumkum stood before Balaram. Raising her hand, she held the revolver over Balaram's head like a sledgehammer.

"Everyone…freeze!" A voice warned from the door.

The 'Inspector' and Kumkum stepped back.

"Anyone who makes the least movement will find his body riddled with holes like a sieve," the voice declared ruthlessly.

Kumkum's hand froze in mid-air. From the corners of her eyes, she could glimpse a police officer.

Gupta and Mangu gaped in shock at the people flooding into the room. Balaram gave a start at the sight of Parabrahma Rao in handcuffs. Rao looked like a standing corpse. Balaram recognized two other members of the contingent – Detective Tempo and Crime Branch Inspector, Pruthvirao. Four armed police personnel stood behind Parabrahma Rao.

"Kumkum, drop your gun! Don't move your hand. Just loosen your fingers!" Tempo warned.

Kumkum instinctively loosened her grip on the revolver and allowed it to fall to the ground.

"Chandidas, the show is over! Raise your hands and turn around," Tempo ordered. "You too, Kumkum!"

Chandidas, the fake Inspector, and Kumkum turned around with fear writ large on their faces.

Inspector Pruthvirao walked towards Chandidas. Roughly thrusting his revolver into the imposter's ribs, he removed the gun in Chandidas's pocket. Tempo picked up Kumkum's revolver, while Pruthvirao handcuffed Chandidas.

"Chandidas, your two disciples outside are safely in our custody, along with the two suitcases. They lost no time in spitting out your name and your past. In fact, your entire biography!" Pruthivirao glared disdainfully at Chandidas, like a real lion looking at a donkey masquerading as a lion. Chandidas looked back fearfully.

"Balaram," remarked Tempo, "you appear to have the gift of choosing accomplices who will double-cross you! It is evident that Kumkum deceived you. Parabrahma Rao, Gajapati and Ramjogi had a grave ready for you in the cellar. Again, the fact that Gupta is not handcuffed indicates that he also sold you out to the fake Inspector Chandidas!"

Balaram's lips trembled as he stared unblinkingly at Tempo. "Gupta is a traitor...he attempted to poison me!"

"You are saddled with duplicitous partners, in line with the duplicate crown you made for your misadventure!" Tempo laughed aloud.

Detective Tempo surveyed the gang which stood like lifeless statues, defeat etched large on their faces – Balaram, Gupta, Mangu, Chandidas, Parabrahma Rao and Kumkum.

"Pruthvirao, make arrangements to transport this band of thieves. Before that, please arrange for the media to cover this as breaking news."

"Mr Tempo, please believe me.... I have not committed any crime..." Gupta whined, only to be cut short by Tempo's guffaw of laughter.

"You have been cleverly maintaining your larger than life image, wearing a mask and taking in the public. But, it was you who advanced the money for this nefarious scheme. Parabrahma Rao and his two friends vouchsafed this information. I am sure that Balaram and Kumkum will also testify to this. You have been a king of thieves all these days and now, you have proved yourself to be a thief!" Tempo declared categorically.

"Tempo," Inspector Pruthvirao extended the phone to him, "the IG wishes to talk to you."

Tempo listened silently to the IG's words and smiled. "No thanks! You can inform the Swamiji over the phone that the crown has been recovered. Inspector Pruthvirao will bring the diamond crown to the ashram…"

He listened on.

"I am sorry, sir! Swamiji's blessings will not put food on the table. I am a private detective and I expect to be recompensed with a reasonable fee for my efforts!"

Tempo smiled and winked at the Inspector.

Towards the Rainbow

A Novel

By Heather L Martin

Cover design by Kylee Martin Lahti

Towards the Rainbow

Copyright @2024 by Heather L Martin

ISBN: 979-8-9906972-0-1